# HEADING WEST
## WESTERN STORIES

# NOEL M. LOOMIS

LEISURE BOOKS  NEW YORK CITY

A LEISURE BOOK®

July 2007

Published by special arrangement with Golden West Literary Agency.

Dorchester Publishing Co., Inc.
200 Madison Avenue
New York, NY 10016

ISBN-10: 0-8439-5897-9
ISBN-13: 978-0-8439-5897-3

The name "Leisure Books" and the stylized "L" with design are trademarks of Dorchester Publishing Co., Inc.

Printed in the United States of America.

Visit us on the web at www.dorchesterpub.com.

# HEADING WEST
## WESTERN STORIES

# TABLE OF CONTENTS

# Foreword

# The Man with the
# Gold-Plated Linotype

The 1950s was a renaissance decade in Western fiction, a period in which much innovative and enduring work was produced by a generation of writers determined to elevate the genre from the slam-bang-action mythos of pulp fiction to historically accurate, character-driven, adult fare. The long and distinguished list of writers who were part of this watershed movement includes Jack Schaefer, Dorothy M. Johnson, Henry W. Allen (Will Henry/Clay Fisher), Les Savage, Jr., T. V. Olsen, Steve Frazee, Wayne D. Overholser, Frank Bonham, Will Cook, and Noel M. Loomis.

Although Noel Loomis (1905–1979) is not quite as well known as some of his peers, his contributions to the maturation of the Western story are significant. One was the introduction of an objective portrayal of violence with neither softening nor melodramatic embellishment. Loomis was both an historian and a newspaperman, and his fictionalized accounts of even the bloodiest episodes in Western history have a lean, reportorial quality that provides intense realism without crossing the line into sensationalism.

His second major contribution was that of painstaking historical accuracy in all aspects of his work. As he wrote in a 1958 article for the Western Writers of America house magazine, *Roundup*: "The illusion of reality is the key to all good writing. Accuracy in Western fiction is not a matter of dates and figures and esoteric data; it is knowing your subject and your background and using it at the proper time." He went on to state that "our only excuse for existing as a field . . . is an accurate portrayal of the West in its deepest sense. Otherwise we might as well dress Buck Rogers in chaps and gun belt and set him to punching cows."

Loomis also believed that "if you can't tell a story, no amount of accuracy will inject life into the writing." He practiced what he preached; he was a fine storyteller as well as a meticulous researcher. Much of his fiction is based on actual events, and all of it is rich in detail and incident and contains a strong illusion of reality. Like Zane Grey, he had the rare ability to see what he called "the color and fire of the West" and to recreate that vision for his readers with all the flair and scope of a Technicolor film.

By his own claim, Noel M(iller) Loomis was born in a newspaper composing room—his mother was a typesetter—in Wakita, Oklahoma Territory. His family was of pioneer stock, one of his grandfathers having taken part in the California Gold Rush and another in the Cherokee Strip Run in 1893. Raised in rough-and-tumble Oklahoma, Texas,

New Mexico, and Wyoming towns where his father, a well-known editor and publisher, worked on local newspapers, Loomis himself took up his parents' trades in his early childhood. He was an accomplished Linotype operator, and once almost single-handedly edited and published a four-page daily in an Oklahoma oil-boom town.

He began writing fiction in the mid-1930s, while newspapering in Minneapolis, and in 1936 made his first professional sale of a short story, "Human Fly," to *Adventure*. The following year he published his first novel, a newspaper mystery titled *Murder Goes to Press*. Two more mysteries were serialized in the Toronto *Star Weekly* in the late 'Thirties, after which he contributed a few Western and several science-fiction tales to pulp magazines, among the latter the well-regarded *City of Glass* (1942). In the years after the close of World War II, his interest in the history and lore of the Old West led him to concentrate exclusively on short stories and fact pieces for such periodicals as *Argosy*, *Adventure*, *Dime Western*, and *Zane Grey's Western Magazine*.

The Western story was his true métier. His first novel in the field, *Rim of the Caprock* (Macmillan, 1952), which dramatically depicts the lives of the ruthless Comancheros who in the 1870s traded with Indians and made their own laws in the Texas Panhandle, was a commercial and critical success; this and subsequent novels established his reputation as a prominent Western writer. Over the next ten years he published nineteen novels, one nonfiction book, and numerous short stories and articles under his own name and the pseudonyms Sam Allison and Frank Miller. He lived in the San Diego, California area during this period and had the curious distinction of being the only professional writer to do all his work on a Linotype machine—that he had salvaged, repaired, installed in his garage workshop, and allegedly had gold-plated. One of the founders of the Western Writers of America in 1953, he served as the organization's second president and later as its secretary-treasurer.

The time frames and subject matter of Loomis's fiction cover nearly two centuries of Western history, from the Revolutionary War era to the 1950s, and, while much of it is set in Texas, most often the Panhandle country known as the *Llano Estacado*, he also used many other locales in the American West and in Mexico. *West to the Sun* (Fawcett Gold Medal, 1955) deals with the *contrabandistas*, vicious outlaws who sold guns to marauding Indians along the Arkansas River in the 1770s. *The Twilighters* (Macmillan, 1955) is his most violent book and yet also his truest for his refusal to water down any of the harsh facts of life in the 1820s among the denizens of the Sabine wilderness, a vast tract of land between Louisiana and New Spain then known as the "Twilight Zone." *Short Cut to Red River* (Macmillan, 1958) is an epic saga of survival based on Henry Connelly's Expedition in 1839, in which a massive wagon train struggled through hostile Comanche territory in order to establish a shortcut trade route from northern Mexico to Arkansas. Texas in the days of the Civil War forms the background for *North to Texas* (Ballantine, 1956), a grim account of the bitter hatred between secessionists and Union sympathizers, and of a plot to sell smuggled quinine, needed by the South to combat rampant malaria among its troops, for a fortune in gold. Also notable is *The Buscadero* (Macmillan, 1953), a spirited tale of a fighting man's efforts to operate a newspaper in a wide-open New Mexico mining town in 1877.

Loomis's short fiction has all the virtues of his longer works. The nine stories collected here demonstrate his versatility, his broad range of interests, his objective realism, and emphasis on historical accuracy and detail. Each is quite different from the others in setting, period, subject matter, character, and tone.

Loomis was one of the few Western writers—Henry W. Allen and Will Cook are two others—who extensively researched Native American cultures and who presented American Indians as distinctive human beings rather than bloodthirsty savages. The first and last stories in these pages display his understanding of, and compassion for, Native Americans. "When the Children Cry for Meat" is the poignant tale of a starving band of Kiowas in 1844, and of the determined efforts of their half-Comanche chief to provide sustenance for his wife and child. "Grandfather Out of the Past," Loomis's second piece of fiction to win a Spur Award from the Western Writers of America—for Best Short Story of 1959—is arguably his *magnum opus*. Packed with fascinating Comanche lore, it concerns an old warrior whose dying time is near, his granddaughter, and the "unclean" brave who seeks to make the young girl one of his wives. Its powerful sexual theme was considered quite daring when the story first appeared, despite the fact that it is handled with restraint and sensitivity.

"The St. Louis Salesman" initially saw print in 1969 and was Loomis's last published Western story. Its protagonist is a dedicated young windmill drummer struggling to sell his wares on the Texas prairie, whose vanquishing of a gang of rustlers with the aid of one of his windmills earns him a pair of satisfying rewards. The building of a railroad through Sonora in the Republic of Mexico requires the leadership of a "Tough *Hombre*," as a John Henryesque steel-drivin' man named Big Blue Buckley proves in a rousing action tale set in 1880. Sly tongue-in-cheek humor is the keynote of "The Stick and the Bearded Lady," and among the ingredients here are a traveling carnival at the close of the 19th Century, counterfeit money, federal agents, and more than one confidence game designed to fleece rodeo cowboys and carny employees.

A young man's coming of age through four years of defeats and bittersweet triumphs on the rodeo circuit comprises the central theme of "The Coming Home," an affecting contemporary yarn set in Wyoming, Montana, and other parts of the West. In complete contrast is the dark and bloody narrative of a brutal band of scalphunters in the 1870s, on the prowl in the Sierra Madres for Apache scalps to sell to the Mexican government, and of the savage retribution visited on their leader by "The Man with No Thumbs."

Logging in the Oregon wilderness in the 1890s forms the background of "The Fighting Road," in which a brash young man learns lessons in friendship, respect, and courage from his father and another hard-shell logger. "Maverick Factory" takes place on the Goodnight-Loving Trail in southeastern Colorado. A cattle drive, a newly married rancher and his well-bred Kansas City wife, a pair of cattle thieves hanged by vigilantes, and a gang operating a rustling dodge known as a "maverick factory" all figure prominently in the plot.

For its contributions to the Western genre, its professional skill, and its entertainment value, the work of Noel M. Loomis merits rediscovery by a new generation of readers. It is to be hoped that *Heading West*, the first collection of his short fiction, will help to bring this about.

Bill Pronzini
Petaluma, California

# When the Children Cry for Meat

In the spring of 1844, Ikämosa's small band of Kiowa Indians was encamped under the east edge of the Caprock in the Texas Panhandle, hopefully awaiting the warmth of a spring already long overdue. Old Ansote, the Kiowa historian, painting his crude symbols on the buffalo hide that bore the Kiowa calendar, had named February "the month the children cried for meat." Doheñte, the ambitious war leader of the band, was restlessly predicting a dry summer with no game at all, and loudly saying that something drastic had to be done. But Ikämosa, the half-Comanche chief of the band, was keeping his concern to himself, hoping to avoid panic, but at the same time worried by a report brought by a Wichita Indian from beyond the *Gañta P'a*, the Double Mountain Fork, that the buffalo had not yet begun to move north because the grass was not turning green.

The Wichita had been in their camp only a short time, and Ikämosa was the only one who could talk his language, so when he relayed the message to the band, he softened it a little to give himself time for thought. The next morning, sitting cross-legged before a small fire of mesquite roots, he pretended to be absorbed in preparations to attach an iron arrow point to a scraped hackberry shaft. He would have preferred a young dogwood shoot, for hackberry required much straightening, but there were few young shoots of anything within range of two days on horseback.

He sensed movement at one side, and then out of the corner of his black eyes he watched T'ene-badaí, Bird Appearing, his third wife, glide down the path toward the creek with their child on her back. T'ene-badaí had hardly sixteen summers, but Ikämosa observed for the first time that her shoulders were thin, and he wondered if she had some mysterious, hidden illness of women. His other two wives had seemed to get along fairly well on the scanty food of the last several months.

He made another turn with the sinew, and Doheñte, No Moccasins, the war leader, came up, nodded gravely, and sat down with considerable ceremony, legs crossed and his heavily beaded leggings, that he had obtained from an American trader, very prominent. He wore his black hair in a long braid down one side, and now his shrewd black eyes in his broad wolf-face stared for an instant at Ikämosa, then darted to T'ene-badaí, who had paused at the chinaberry tree to shake the sand out of her moccasins. There was a question in his eyes that Ikämosa did not understand, but he went ahead with his wrapping. Doheñte, turning his attention to the fire, observed: "Our wives have trouble finding enough snakes and tortoises to keep from starving."

"It is true," said Ikämosa, involuntarily looking toward T'ene-badaí, who was on her knees with her hands in the water. He pulled his thoughts back to Doheñte. He puffed slowly on the pipe and then handed it to the war leader; this was an informal smoke, and it was not necessary to observe the ritual. He glanced at Doheñte's long braid; it was whispered that Doheñte had married his fourth wife just to get her hair to add to his own.

"I have not found game," Ikämosa admitted, "because I thought that any day the buffalo would be here, that it was not necessary to look very far." He gazed up at the great, forbidding, purple-and-brown palisade that to all Plains Indians meant the *Pasañgya*, the Edge Prairie, the *Llano Estacado*. "Even the mustangs and the antelope have not appeared."

"The grass on the *Pasañgya* does not grow without water," Doheñte pointed out. "And this winter we have had much cold but little snow."

Ikämosa took the pipe back. "True," he said.

"Without grass," Doheñte went on, "there will be few prairie dogs and fewer rabbits, and coyotes will go to other parts of the country. Deer and antelope and buffalo will not be here, and the bears will migrate. There will not even be *takiadl* . . . prairie chickens."

That was sarcasm, for the Kiowas did not like any kind of fowl, and Ikämosa grunted.

Doheñte seemed intent on driving home the dismal forecast: "It does not seem that there will be anything to eat this summer but skunks and horned toads."

Ikämosa shuddered. Skunks were always bad medicine, and he said thoughtfully: "Unless we move the band to another place."

"Where could we go?" Doheñte demanded.

Ikämosa was silent. This valley along the *Tóñ-zogódal P'a*, the Swift Water River where the Tehaneko had been massacred three years before, had been an ideal camping place for many years.

Ikämosa tried to sort out the truths from Doheñte's insistent words. Doheñte was a year older, and Ikämosa, seeing the hostility in Doheñte's eyes, knew for the first time that Doheñte was jealous of his position as chief. Doheñte was a good war leader, but, when he was not on the trail, he was a constant troublemaker. But Ikämosa restrained his tongue, and watched T'ene-badaí come back up the trail with a rawhide container filled with water. She glanced at him briefly, and he thought there was a hunger in her eyes, but he could not read them further, for she looked at the ground again, and bent far over as she trudged up the incline to her tent.

Ikämosa turned suddenly and caught Doheñte's beady eyes on T'ene-badaí's back as she disappeared into the teepee.

Doheñte said: "Your third wife has grown into a woman."

"Yes," Ikämosa said shortly, and his tone forbade Doheñte's pursuit of the subject, for Doheñte's interest in women was well known.

Doheñte pointed at the brass kettle with the stem of the pipe. "Your father did not have such a convenience as that, but ate his meat raw, or singed a little on the coals."

"For my taste," said Ikämosa thoughtfully, "it was better meat, cooked that way. Boiled meat has little flavor."

Doheñte's eyes dropped, and he picked up the former conversation: "Nevertheless, you have found items like that brass kettle very useful."

"It is worth nothing empty," said Ikämosa.

"It need not be empty," said Doheñte, extending the pipe.

Ikämosa took the pipe and looked at the fire. "I do not know how you expect to put food in it when there is none to be had," he said.

Doheñte watched Ikämosa sharply. "Man-henk'-ia . . . the *Hañpóko* known as No Arm, from Bent's Fort," he said, "is building a trading post on the *P'o P'a* . . . Beaver Creek. He sends word to all Indians to trade there with him, and promises to have flour, cornmeal, dried meat, sugar, salt, tobacco, and coffee. Tobacco . . . not willow bark," he said scornfully. "And coffee!" he exclaimed. "I have not had real coffee all winter . . . nothing but roasted acorns from the *Gañta P'a*."

"Nor have I," said Ikämosa, choosing his words carefully. "But we agreed when we formed this band that we would not trade with the *Hañpóko*, the Americans, except for powder and balls."

"It is true," said Doheñte, "but I cannot bear to see my wives and children go hungry. I hear their sobbing in the night."

*Or, rather,* thought Ikämosa, *you are thinking of hot coffee in that well-padded stomach.* He put aside the thought of hot coffee, for it made his own stomach growl. He said: "We have had no meat for weeks . . . nothing but a few wild potatoes that my women found up under the Caprock . . . and those hardly made one kettleful."

"Then it is agreed," said Doheñte, rising. "We shall go to Man-henk'ia. The women and children will be glad!"

But Ikämosa did not stir. "We have nothing to trade . . . no white iron, no yellow iron, no hides or skins."

"Man-henk'ia will trust us until winter."

"And charge us three prices. It is an old trick of the *Hañpóko*."

"It is their way," said Doheñte, "and beggars cannot be choosers."

"We are not beggars," Ikämosa said levelly, and knocked the ashes out of his pipe against the rock. "It means our women will work for him next fall and winter, preparing skins. It means that we shall have to get still more flour and coffee from him, and vermilion and beads and ribbons, and brass kettles. . . ." He stood up. "And then Man-henk'ia will own us because he will own all our work for years to come."

"You cannot object to food," said Doheñte.

"If we get it this way. I don't like the things that come with it," Ikämosa said stubbornly. "The Kiowas have always been free to come and go. Sometimes we have been hungry, but we have depended on our own efforts to get food . . . and we have always gotten it."

"New things, good things, brought to our country . . ."

Ikämosa stood up. "New things, good things are no better because we can reach across a counter and take them . . . especially when we shall have to work for months to pay for them. The men had it right," he said. "The *Hañpóko* come among us with things we do not need, and make us want them, and then make us work to buy them."

"Man-henk'ia is there when the buffalo are not," Doheñte observed shrewdly.

"It is true," said Ikämosa. "And always with his hand out, and always with invisible bands like ropes of deer sinew that tie us to him and his mud teepee."

Doheñte said shrewdly: "Your wives' parents will think badly of you if you do not provide for them when it is as easy as this."

Ikämosa looked at him. "In a matter like this, I will make my own decision. The parents are not involved."

Doheñte did not seem discouraged, and Ikämosa wondered what he was holding back. He wondered, too, why Doheñte was so insistent. "Rather than trade our wives' work and eventually their bodies to Man-henk'ia," Ikämosa said, "we can send scouts in all directions to find game, and then move to the place where it is."

Doheñte's eyes took on a strange glint. "Then you refuse?" he asked.

"I think there is a better way," said Ikämosa.

Doheñte said casually: "Some predicted you would say that."

"You have discussed it, then?"

Doheñte shrugged. "A little."

"How do the others feel?"

Doheñte seemed studiously absorbed in the fire. "Some said that because your mother was a Comanche slave, you would not care whether the Kiowas starve or not."

Ikämosa drew a sudden deep breath. "I was raised a Kiowa," he said, "but I have never lost the Comanche's love of coming and going as he wishes."

"But, of course, I told them," said Doheñte, "that since your father was a Kiowa chief, and since you were raised a Kiowa, of course you are interested in nothing but the welfare of the band."

Ikämosa said flatly: "You came here to force a showdown. That is plain. You will start campaigning against me now, and one of us will have to leave the band. You had that in mind when you walked up here." For a moment his annoyance got the better of him. "Leave my fire or I will throw you in it," he said.

Doheñte's black eyes glinted. "Perhaps they were right . . . perhaps you are more Comanche than Kiowa." He rose and walked away.

Ikämosa watched his horny feet send out little spats of dust as he walked away. For some reason, Doheñte had his mind set on trading with Man-henk'ia, and Ikämosa knew that he would talk to every warrior in the tribe—and perhaps even to the women—to convince them that it was best.

Ikämosa heard a soft step behind him, and turned to look at T'ene-badaí. She met his eyes briefly and stepped to the kettle. "I found a frog," she said, and dropped it into the simmering water.

He shuddered. Frogs were worse than snakes.

"It is food," she said, "and your flesh hangs like wet rags on your big bones."

He put out a hand to stop her as she started to leave. "You are not happy with me," he said.

For the first time in weeks, she looked at him squarely. "You have never made me unhappy," she said.

He frowned. "Your eyes have been downcast for a long time."

"Perhaps."

"Do you want to go back to your parents?"

She eyed him levelly. "I am a woman now. I would not go back to my father's teepee."

He said slowly: "You might have come to me against your will."

She was scornful. "You forget that my father is the son of Zép-ko-éte, and he never sold any of his daughters unless they wanted to go."

Yes, he remembered now. And he remembered, also, that he and she had stood together many evenings beyond the firelight; he remembered her laughing black eyes, and how she had grown to womanhood at his very touch. Yes, he remembered. "But what has happened now?" he asked.

She said softly, her eyes on the ground: "I knew that you and I were right for each other, and I was glad, but I did not know or think . . . I was too inexperienced to realize that your other wives would not allow us to have each other."

It hit him with staggering force that he had taken it for granted that his other wives would be kind to her, and that he had not given it a second thought—and the joy had fled from her eyes.

"I do not complain," she said. "This is the way of the Kiowas."

He realized he could not complain, either. He re-

membered the quiet, delightfully sweet days of
their first week, away from the band, up near the
Caprock; early summer evenings whose caress-
ingly mild breezes had wafted over them the sweet
fragrance of mesquite blossoms while they talked
and while they loved. Then they had come back
with the band, and T'ene-badaí had been installed
in her own teepee, but he realized now that his
other wives, Dämätána and Agabia, had begun to
make demands on him, and presently he had once
again been drawn into the affairs of the band and
into the circle of his own family, while T'ene-badaí
had been pushed further and further into the background. He knew, too, as he looked at her honest
eyes, that he had bought his first two wives to take
care of his teepee and his medicine and his
honors—and they had been well satisfied; but he
had taken T'ene-badaí because there had been
something in her eyes especially for him. He had
never admitted that to anybody, for it would have
been unmanly, but he was keenly aware of it now,
and it did not seem entirely reprehensible to him.

He heard the voices of his other two wives coming across the village from their parents' home, and
it struck him for a moment that they sounded like a
flock of hen turkeys. But he put the thought behind
him. They had been wives in all that he had asked
of them; perhaps they had no more capacity to be
wives. Perhaps, he thought for a fleeting second,
they were not even women yet, whereas T'ene-
badaí, hardly more than half the age of Dämätána,
had grown into a woman before his eyes.

He was glad that T'ene-badaí also heard the
voices of the older women, lowered her eyes, and

went back to her teepee. A moment later, as he was sitting down before the fire preparing to make the deer-hoof glue to fasten the feathers on the arrow, he heard their baby wail plaintively, and he knew that T'ene-badaí was trying to nurse it from her pitifully thin breasts that held hardly more than enough milk to wet its lips. And for a moment his heart went out to them both, and he felt heavily on his shoulders the burden of their hunger.

Then his other wives were there and swept past him without noticing him and without speaking to him. Their voices rose as they discussed the new trading post of Man-henk'ia, and obviously they were excited about it.

He sat there for a while, hearing the low wail of T'ene-badai's baby. Finally it bothered him so that he went to the teepee and stood for a moment until his eyes became accustomed to the darkness, and he could make out T'ene-badaí with the child in her arms. He suddenly felt an uncontrollable hunger for her, but her eyes were down, and the exquisite poignancy of his desire settled into a dull, throbbing thing confused with a great many other feelings that he could not sort out.

One thing was clear, however. "I will get meat for you," he said.

She looked up at last, and there was no hostility in her eyes. "Do not do anything you do not want to do," she said.

He turned away in time to see Bäo, the wrinkled father of Dämätána and Agabia, walk up to his fire.

They went through the formalities, and then Bäo

said: "Doheñte reports you are opposed to our getting supplies from Man-henk'ia."

Ikämosa nodded, his eyes on Bäo's.

"Both my daughters are in favor," said Bäo.

Ikämosa said: "I thought they would be."

"There is no use being stubborn," Bäo went on. "If the *Hañpóko* is willing to furnish us things on credit, why should we not accept them?"

Ikämosa looked at him, but made no attempt to answer.

"What can you do?" Bäo demanded.

"I can find meat," said Ikämosa.

"The band will not follow you."

"That is something we do not know."

"Doheñte will not follow you."

Ikämosa nodded. He had expected that. "And you?" he asked.

Bäo hesitated, then said: "If my daughters want to go with you . . . but they, too, must eat."

"I have noticed," said Ikämosa, "that their shoulders are well filled out." It occurred to him then that they might secretly have been getting food from the *Hañpóko*, but it was a disloyal thought, and he put it out of his mind. "If they are attracted to the *Hañpóko*," he said slowly, "it is because of beads and ribbons."

"A woman is entitled to pretty things, isn't she?"

"She is," said Ikämosa, realizing with a pang that T'ene-badaí had had very few pretty things. "But it is a question whether she should trade her birthright for them."

Old Bäo's black eyes looked from a wrinkled face. "Are you, then, opposed to Man-henk'ia?"

"I do not think it wise."

Bäo said: "There will be a meeting tonight, at which all the warriors will have a chance to talk, and the decision will be made."

Ikämosa nodded. He had just caught a whiff of the cooking frog, and it smelled good. Old Bäo also smelled it, and looked into the kettle with distaste. "Is this what you are providing your family to eat . . . this . . . this *kadlei-kyadlei?*" he asked.

Ikämosa did not answer, did not nod, and presently old Bäo went away. Then Ikämosa fished the frog out of the simmering water and took it to T'ene-badaí.

"I cannot," she said. "You have a big body, and it needs much more food than mine."

For a moment her eyes were soft, and he was touched. His hand rested lightly on her shoulder. "Then eat it for the milk it will produce," he said, and left it with her.

It was the greatest meeting ever held by Ikämosa's band. All forty-two of his warriors were there, sitting in the first rows around the fire. Ikämosa took his usual place at the head of the circle. The women were sitting scattered behind the men, and beyond, half in darkness, the children were playing, some running, occasionally shouting or shrieking. Ikämosa got settled, feeling the hostility against him, and took his time starting the pipe, while Doheñte sprinkled sage on the fire as a purifying incense.

Ikämosa dipped the pipe toward the four corners of the compass, and blew out puffs of smoke for the Sun and the Earth and the Moon. Then he passed the pipe to old Bäo, who went through approximately the same routine before handing the pipe to Doheñte. It would be some time before the pipe would get all the way around, and they could begin the talk, so Ikämosa looked for his wives. He saw Dämätána and Agabia sitting with their mothers. He looked for T'ene-badaí, but could not find her. She was not with her parents, and he could not see her anywhere within the light of the fire. He wondered where she was and what she was doing.

Presently Doheñte started the talk about Manhenk'ia, the *Hañpóko*. Ikämosa pointed out their original agreement, but Doheñte said that Manhenk'ia had been known to them a long time and had been a friend. Bäo echoed Doheñte's arguments, and then, one at a time, the other warriors spoke on the matter, each one taking up time according to his importance in the tribe.

It was after midnight before each one had spoken. By that time it was clear that they were united against Ikämosa. Doheñte had done his work well, for not a single voice was raised against the thought of dependence on the trading post for their future supplies.

After the last man had finished, Ikämosa filled and lit the pipe again—the fragrant willow bark— and went through the same ritual, and then started it around the circle. He had to have time to think, to decide whether he should accede to the wishes of the others, or whether he would adhere to the long-standing rule—the precept of his father. It was not an easy decision. His own feelings were strong, but they were all he had to support him against the combined opinions of the band. Eventually he had to speak, to say his thoughts, to act as chief. He put the pipe down and fixed his gaze on the fire, asking for guidance from his medicine, for wisdom to know the best course, for strength to follow it.

"The majority . . . in fact, everyone here except me . . . wants to trade with Man-henk'ia," he said, "and it would be a stubborn chief who would not listen to the wishes of the people."

Old Bäo smiled thinly, and Doheñte had a satisfied smirk on his bronze face, but Ikämosa ignored them, for the only thing that mattered was the right decision. "It is against my judgment," he said, "but it may, after all, be the best decision." He sat up straighter, listening, and on the night wind he heard it again—the faint wail of his and T'ene-badaí's child.

Old Bäo heard it, too, and was quick to take advantage of it. "Your own child needs milk," he said, "but there cannot be milk without food."

But Ikämosa was thinking of something else, of T'ene-badaí, who was not sitting with any of them, not even with her own mother. The shocking thought came to him that perhaps T'ene-badaí, hungering for food and for the bright ornaments of the *Hañpóko*, had already left the camp and left their baby behind. It blinded him for a moment, and he closed his eyes until the shock passed. Then he opened his eyes and reached again for the pipe. He made the usual salutations, but when he finished, he put the pipe back on the stone to indicate he had come to a decision, that there would be no further talk.

He looked up and saw old Bäo's shrewd eyes on him, saw Doheñte's cynical face, and suddenly knew what Doheñte's interest was: special favors from the trader. He looked around the circle, searching each face in turn. The older ones were harder to read; the very young ones were difficult to interpret, but he saw many whose motivations were plain: acquiescence to the wishes of their wives, an easier life, and perhaps, in some, a little avarice—a hope that they could somehow get more than somebody else.

"The *Hañpóko* are as numerous as the leaves on a *qua-hei peip* . . . a mesquite bush," said old Bäo. "It is bound to come sooner or later."

Ikämosa drew a deep breath. "I am not going to give in to it." He looked straight at Doheñte. "I am not going with you. My family and I will go to look for another *kadl-hia* . . . buffalo. If the buffalo will not come to us, we will go to them."

Old Bäo glared at him, outraged. Doheñte's thin lips were drawn up in a smirk. There was utter silence for a moment.

"The Tonkawas will be after you," said Doheñte. "They will take your wives and eat your children."

Ikämosa knew that Doheñte was merely putting on face, that he would be glad to get rid of Ikämosa, because, with Ikämosa gone, Doheñte, who was leading this move, would be elected chief. Ikämosa thought to himself: *This band will turn into coffee-coolers sitting around the post—little better than beggars.* "I can fight the Tonkawas," he said aloud, "and I am not afraid." He knew what Doheñte had been saying against him, and he threw it in their faces, honoring the memory of his mother at the same time: "I am half Comanche. I am not afraid."

There was a moment of silence, and old Bäo said finally: "Your wives will not go with you."

"My wives will go where I go."

"Your first two wives are my daughters," said Bäo slowly. "They will not go."

Ikämosa concealed his start. So they had already decided. Turning his head slowly, he looked at Dämätána and Agabia, sitting near their father's teepee. They stared at him without change of expression, without any evidence of friendliness—and he knew, as he turned back, that they, too, were against him, that the ribbons and beads of Man-henk'ia were more important to them than the privilege of coming and going as they wished; that the ease of making a trip to the trading post and returning with food that would not have to be paid for until next winter was more important to them than anything else. He felt, also, that if those two, who had had the best of his efforts, were ready to desert him, then T'ene-badaí also would go with the band, for she had far less of material possessions than they had.

It frightened him for a moment, and he wondered if he had spoken hastily. He looked at the warriors around him—at Doheñte, who was so determined to have his way; at Ansote, the historian, who had said nothing, but who was getting old himself and perhaps foresaw an easier life where a man would not have to mount and ride whenever game was not in sight or food was scarce; at the ancient Giákaíte, who could no longer ride or hunt and whose eyes were too dim for him even to make arrows, and who had nothing to look forward to under normal circumstances except perhaps, one day in the coming summer, being left in the middle of the *Pasañgya* with a bag of mesquite meal, to die of starvation; at Set-dayáite, who still had many horses and six wives—one from each of the families of influence; at Pa-tepte, who was half Mexican and who had a nagging wife; at Mápódal, Split Nose, the father of T'ene-badaí, who also was old and hoping to avoid the common end; at all the others whose impassive, uncompromising stares told him their feelings. The power of the tribal opinion was frightening, massive, smothering, and he began to weaken. Then he looked at Doheñte's horny feet, and for the first time he understood Doheñte, whose lifelong refusal to wear moccasins had been a defiance of the tribal customs. For the first time, Ikämosa understood that that defiance had not been for a good purpose, but rather to attract attention.

He felt the tribal pulse beat in his wrists, and he fought to throw it off. Suddenly, in pure Comanche fashion, he resented being forced. He straightened up and looked at them all. "If you want to be coffee-coolers . . . to sit around the trader's post and drink his coffee and pretend to be wise and agreeable when he is selling you things you don't need for things you haven't got, it is a great thing. But tomorrow, when some trader will build a post a little closer . . . perhaps on the *Iyúgua P'a*, and maybe he will have alcohol, and you will have become dependent on his goods, and you will go there for them, and, while you are there, you will taste the alcohol, and you will lose control of your senses . . . and when you wake up, like the Tonkawas, you will have drunk up all your skins for the next winter, and then you will not have any left to buy the beads and the ribbons that your wives now want." He looked at them, sitting around him so impassively, and suddenly, for a moment, he was angry. "But maybe," he shouted, "you will not any longer need those beads and ribbons, because maybe in your drunkenness you will have killed your wives and left their bones unburied." He stopped for a moment to cool off.

Old Bäo must have been a little uncertain, for he offered a last defense: "You are not like us, anyway. You are half Comanche."

"Yes, I am half Comanche," spoke Ikämosa, "and I am not afraid to go alone." He spoke to Ansote across the fire. "I respect your age and position as historian, but you can look a long way back, and you must know that I speak the truth. It may well be that the *Hañpóko* with their barrels of food have prayed away the rain so that we should be forced to trade with them. I do not know. It may be that the *Hañpóko* with their beads and their ribbons have made our wives dissatisfied so that we shall be forced to promise our next year's skins to keep our wives from complaining. I do not know. But I do know this!" He paused and looked around the circle, till finally his gaze stopped on Doheñte. "I know that every time we use something the *Hañpóko* sells, we create a hunger for it, and we have to go back and get more of it . . . and I know that we can get those things nowhere else, and so after a while we don't like to go too far away, and the game gets still more scarce, and then we are the slaves of those who have the goods we do not need."

Of them all, only Ansote seemed alarmed. The rest had been well prepared by Doheñte. But Ansote muttered: "It is a mistake."

"The price of doing right," Ikämosa said, "is always ten times as high when a man has to fight his own people. When they are not sure, they want to force everybody else to do the same, so they will all be in the same fix. The price is high," he repeated, "but I am going to pay it. I shall go today . . . within the hour, when the sky turns light in the east. If I must go alone, I will go alone."

He stood up and waited for an answer, but there was none. "I am going to find the buffalo," he said. "When I do, I will send word. By that time, some of you may have found out what it is like to belong to the *Hañpóko*, and you may want to live like men again." He strode from the fire, sad at their shortsightedness, but weighted down with uncertainty in spite of his brave words. He had lost everything: his wives and children, his band, his chieftanship. He was alone, and it was a terrible feeling.

He reached his fire and saw the brass kettle still in place. But his teepee was down—down and packed upon his horses. He felt a glad rush of exaltation, for T'ene-badaí was waiting, her baby on her back. She was going with him, and that was enough for the moment, because his heart was oppressed over the hostility of the tribe, and the frightening realization that he was leaving the band and going to an unknown place.

They set out in silence, and no one came to watch them leave. He went ahead, leading his four horses, and T'ene-badaí walked behind, her eyes on the ground, her mule following her. He led the way to the south, and they camped that night near a gyppy spring that he would not allow her to drink from. He saw her eyes on him once, but he was still too full of hurt and uncertainty to speak to her.

They went on the next day into a wildly broken country of steep hills, many scattered rocks, and dense underbrush; they camped that night without water and without food. They continued south on the third day, and the country got worse for traveling; they found water but no game. On the fourth day it was the same. On the fifth day he knew from T'ene-badaí's ashen face that she could not go on much farther. On that day they found honey in a hollow pecan tree, and he realized that they were lost, and perhaps in Tonkawa country.

He had been so depressed by the knowledge that he had been rejected by his people for being steadfast in his principles that he had hardly looked at T'ene-badaí for the first two days. Then the heaviness had begun to wear off, replaced by the dire need for water, and then by the steady, day-after-day absence of game, the constant, growing hunger pains, and the harsh knowledge that their plight was desperate.

He made the small fire that night in silence. He watched his wife nurse their child at dry breasts, and heard its tiny wail of hunger during the night.

On the sixth morning he was awake at dawn, and perhaps, he thought, he was about to die of starvation, for a great deal of the hurt and the fear and the uncertainty was gone, and in their place had come a feeling of peace. He thought of T'ene-badaí then, and looked over at her and found her eyes wide, watching his. He said: "They never did let you have enough to eat, did they?"

She shrugged. "It was their way," she said.

He knew. Envy and jealousy were common among Indian women, and he should have watched. "I . . ."

She glanced past his shoulder, and her eyes widened. She whispered in a very low voice: "There is a *kadl-hia* in the valley, half a mile down."

He froze for an instant, then looked. Buffalo! His mind added up all the factors in a flash. His buffalo horse, the *takoñ*, the black-eared horse, was grazing with the mule ridden by T'ene-badaí. Ikämosa slid silently out of his bed, put his killing knife in the waistband of his breechclout, slipped over to the grazing animals like a shadow in the early morning, and stood up when the horse was between him and the buffalo. Careful not to disturb the horse, he slid on it without a bridle. She was somehow beside him, soundless, and put his lance in his hand. In the dim light he touched her face and let his fingers stay there for a moment. He looked down at her thin face, and realized his own weakness, and closed his eyes for a moment to implore his power for strength and skill and courage. Then he urged the horse forward at a walk, keeping low on its side opposite the buffalo, his leg hooked over the horse's withers, his eyes watching the *kadl-hia* from under the horse's neck.

The buffalo was a big one—an old bull, cast out by the younger bulls, and therefore it had been feeding alone and was in good shape. The horse went steadily closer. The bull looked up, its black, curved horns silhouetted against the eastern sky; then, not seeing Ikämosa, it went back to grazing.

The horse was almost alongside before the buffalo got Ikämosa's scent and whirled. The horse had expected that, and dodged backward to evade the horns. Then it swung around the buffalo and came up behind at a hard gallop. Ikämosa yelled as the buffalo straightened out; he wanted it to run. It became confused, and did run, and the *takoñ* drew alongside, its hoofs pounding in the soft grass. But fifty yards ahead was a thick growth of chaparral, and, if the buffalo could make it, the horse would not be able to follow. Ikämosa pounded the horse with his left hand as it drew up on the buffalo's right side; then he leaned far over and drove the point of the lance with all his might into the soft spot behind the shoulder blade. The lance went deep, through the lungs and somewhere near the heart. The buffalo staggered, then regained its balance, wheeled to the left, and pounded up the valley, the long lance bobbing from its back.

Ikämosa stopped the horse and watched the buffalo go. If chased, the animal would stay on its feet for hours, even though the lance should be in a vital spot; but if not followed, it would surely die—if the lance should be in a vital spot. Ikämosa looked up and saw T'ene-badaí a short distance away, watching.

The lance got caught off balance and snapped in two. Then the bull turned in a half circle and came back down the valley, running like a red-eyed demon. Blood was streaming from its mouth, but its head was still in normal position. It went past without seeing him, and Ikämosa wheeled the *takoñ* and went after it, now uncertain of his catch. If the buffalo should be so crazed as to run for a long time, the horse would not be able to keep it in sight; the *takoñ*, now in fair shape because it had not been ridden, might run for two or three hours, but no more. There was no doubt that the bull was crazy with fear and pain—such an animal was the hardest to kill.

Ikämosa drew his knife as the *takoñ* pulled up on the left side this time. The buffalo swerved and ran with new speed, and suddenly Ikämosa's fear of losing the meat came over him, and he felt momentarily faint; then the *takoñ* was alongside once more, and Ikämosa leaned far over and began to cut at the buffalo like a man possessed. He went in through the soft spot ahead of its hip bone, and the sharp knife worked fast while the bull seemed not to feel the pain in its already crazed brain.

Ikämosa dug deeply with the knife, slashed here and there furiously; he put both hands in the hole and came up with a steaming kidney. He slid off the horse, for he knew the bull could not go far now, and stared at the hot, bloody kidney for a moment while the old hunger went over him like a weakening pain. For one moment he held the kidney aloft to show his power that he was appreciative of its help; then he buried his face in the kidney and bit out a huge chunk of steaming meat and swallowed it whole. He trembled and took a second bite, and then remembered his wife. She was coming on the mule, and he ran to her and handed her the kidney without a word.

The buffalo was slowing down; it would stop, he felt sure, by the time it reached the stream. He did not want to alarm it and inspire it to renewed efforts, so he stayed for a moment, watching it, while he and T'ene-badaí finished the hot kidney. They washed in the creek, and he went after the bull, which by now was on its knees, its head pendulous, its chin whiskers brushing the earth.

Four buzzards were overhead, and a coyote was standing in the edge of the chaparral, but Ikämosa cut the buffalo's throat, and presently they had it skinned and the meat piled on the hide. T'ene-badaí went back for horses, and they took the meat to camp. By that time, they were ravishingly hungry, and ate again; hump ribs and leaf fat—all raw. They had a fire going, and began to make racks out of willow branches to dry the meat. Then they were hungry, and ate again.

They ate and worked all day and into the night. They ate smoked tongue, raw liver, small intestines. Before it was over, they had eaten twenty pounds of meat apiece—and for the first time in months their stomachs were full. Already the meat had produced milk in T'ene-badaí's small body, and her brown breasts, once shrunken, now were full and ripe, and the baby nursed eagerly, and, when it had finished, no longer cried.

Toward the second dawn they had all the meat on racks; it would take another day and night to dry it, and one of them would have to stay awake to keep the animals away. But in the meantime they would eat fresh meat until they could hold no more. Ikämosa looked at T'ene-badaí across the fire. Her eyes were open, and he recognized the age-old question in them.

But something worried him. "You could have stayed with the band," he said, "and you could have been sure."

She smiled in the soft West Texas dawn. "I told my father to sell me to you because I wanted to be your wife."

"Wouldn't you rather," he asked, "be sure of food every day?"

"If we are hungry today, we will have food tomorrow," she said. "I am not afraid when I am with you."

He saw the question again in her eyes, and he got up and went around the fire. She was on her feet to meet him, and he took her hungrily but gently into his arms.

# The St. Louis Salesman

Dick Marshall was far from the city, holding the reins on his first team in the middle of a vast, mesquite-covered prairie. The team was no trouble, for it walked along steadily. They were livery-stable animals and looked a little mangy, it seemed to him, but then he was no expert on horseflesh. They were horses, and they had done whatever Dick Marshall had wanted them to do. So far.

However, he had other worries than the horses: he was down to $1.90, and he was heading into ranch country where he knew nobody personally. His stiff straw hat was no trouble, for it walked along his head, although the black ribbon that had one end fastened to the lapel of his black-and-white-checked coat and which was supposed to keep the hat from being blown away—they were very natty in St. Louis—had come loose, and he had left it draped over a clump of beargrass.

He counted the money again and felt in his pockets for a stray five-dollar gold piece, but found none.

Nevertheless, he still sat straight on the spring seat of the wagon, for his sales manager had said: "No matter how low you get, keep up the front, boy!"

He watched the endless mesquite go by, and reflected gloomily that he wouldn't be able to keep up the front much longer unless he should make a sale. He looked behind him to make sure his cargo was intact. The various boxes contained one Western Zephyr windmill, ready to be sold. The windmill wheel was packed in a tall crate on the left side of the wagon bed, and he was reassured to see that the boxes had not changed position since he had loaded them into the wagon at the freight depot with the help of a townsman who had walked down to see the train come in. Now he turned back to the road. The sun was hot, and the alkali dust was caked on his parched lips. Then a sleek, brown, long-legged bird about half as big as a young pullet darted out of the mesquite bushes and took off down the road in front of the team.

Dick Marshall sat up. The roadrunner turned its head sidewise and looked back. Marshall recognized the challenge, and sat forward and slapped the reins on his team's rumps. The horses began to trot, and the wagon began to rumble. The roadrunner speeded up with no apparent effort. The liveryman had warned him not to make the horses go faster than a walk, but Marshall fingered the buggy whip. The roadrunner looked back again, and Marshall was stirred by the joy of battle. There was nothing ahead but endless miles of flat country and an enormous light-blue sky with a single wind-whipped cloud. He jammed his straw hat harder on his head, pulled the whip out of the socket, and laid it on the team.

The horses lunged into a heavy gallop.

"Go git 'em!" he yelled through the dust. He stood up in the wagon box and applied the whip, while the windmill, fresh with paint, bounced around in the back of the wagon. Then the left front wheel of the wagon hit a mesquite root, and the windmill-wheel crate lurched and went over the side with a groan of nailed boards.

"Whoa!" yelled Marshall, suddenly scared.

He jerked rudely on the reins. The roadrunner looked back with a saucy toss of his head and veered off into the mesquite, while the sweating horses plowed to a stop, sawing against the bits. Marshall, now sober, wrapped the reins around the iron and climbed down from the wagon.

He walked back down the road; the windmill wheel was in the middle of a clump of mesquite and not injured. He began to wrestle with it, but realized that he'd better back the wagon to it. He sawed on the reins and commanded the team to—"Back up!"—but the horses did not seem to understand.

Then a clear girl's voice with just a tinkle of amusement asked: "Having trouble?"

Dick Marshall sat up straight and tried to look at her, but for a few seconds his sight was bothered by a number of questions—where had she been?—why would a girl be out here anyway?—would she report him to the liveryman?

Her voice came clearly: "Don't you know the livery stable will charge you double for running the horses?"

"How will they know?" he asked.

She pointed to the white salt on the heaving sides.

Marshall shrugged.

She came closer. "I used to do that when I was a kid . . . until my daddy spanked me for it."

Somehow a pearl-handled revolver in a brass-studded gun belt came into his vision, and he looked up at her face. The girl was on a beautiful bay that made his livery-stable team look moth-eaten. She had chestnut-brown hair, tied in a prim knot at the back of her neck, and she had deep blue eyes that appraised his curly brown hair quite frankly.

Dick Marshall swallowed. He had supposed a girl who could ride a horse would be sort of horse-faced and leather-skinned, but this one wasn't. She had a very clear white skin with two spots of nice red high up on her cheekbones. He took off his hat. "Miss," he said, "would you like to buy a windmill?"

She rode around him and examined him as if she were buying a horse. "Are you headed for the Walking H Ranch?" she asked finally.

"Where else does this road go?"

She sat back in the saddle. Her man's shirt fit her very snugly across the chest. "It might go back to town if you keep chasing roadrunners," she said.

He remembered his manners. "I'm Dick Marshall from Saint Louis," he said. "I haven't had the pleasure . . ."

"I'm Joan Brainerd," she said, looking straight into his eyes.

"Brainerd!" He stared. Her father must be the one who owned the Walking H—all fifty sections!

"If you want your team backed," she said, "I'll do it for you."

"I'd be obliged," he said. "That's one thing they didn't include in my training."

She dismounted very smoothly, put one slim, booted foot on the axle, and sort of floated into the wagon. At least, it seemed so. She sat very straight on the seat and began to work the reins and talk to the horses. The team backed until the wagon was beside the crate that held the windmill wheel.

She draped the reins over the dashboard and jumped down lightly; the knot of red hair lifted a little, when she jumped, and then dropped back against her neck when she landed. "Now," she said, "I'll help you get the thing back into the wagon."

He didn't think it was exactly woman's work, but she had hold of the box, and there they were, side by side, heaving the box into the wagon. Her foot slid off the mesquite root, and she fell against him and for a second seemed to rest there. She was warm and solid and vital. He saw that her face was flushed, and he held up his side of the box while she recovered.

They shoved the box inside. She snapped up the tailgate and dropped in the hasp.

"You sure know your wagon," he said admiringly.

She looked at him, but he could not read her blue eyes.

"Would you care to drive the rest of the way for me?" he asked.

A moment later they were sitting on the spring seat with the team in a slow walk while the big bay strode majestically behind the wagon, his reins tied to the tailgate. It was very pleasant, watching Miss Brainerd from the side, for she sat very straight.

"So you are hauling a windmill, Mister Marshall," she said presently.

"I'm going to demonstrate it to your father," he said.

"A windmill?"

"It pumps water for cattle to drink," he explained.

"Will it really work?"

"It's what this country west of the Mississippi needs most. It will pump water all day long on a breath of air."

"Well," she said, "it will get a strong breath out here on the South Plains." She glanced at him. "Why are you going to demonstrate it to my father?"

"I want to sell it to him," said Dick Marshall.

There was a hint of coolness in her voice. "Are you . . . a salesman?"

His sales manager had said—"Never be ashamed of your profession."—and he answered: "Yes." The truth was, of course, that he didn't know whether he was or not because he hadn't sold a windmill yet.

"A traveling salesman?" she insisted.

Marshall heard the warning. "I've just come from Saint Louis," he said cautiously.

"We shot the last traveling salesman through the left ear," she said thoughtfully.

Marshall straightened.

"Father doesn't like traveling salesmen. He says they act as if they come out here to save the world.

And they talk too much. They don't give him time to think."

Marshall rose to his own defense. "A salesman has to talk."

She answered: "He doesn't have to be obnoxious."

Marshall was getting annoyed because, for one thing, the conversation was not going the way it was supposed to go. Just because she had red-gold hair, she needn't . . . "You must realize," he said, "that the world is moving right along, and selling is an integral part of modern business. I've got something you need, and I'm doing you a favor by showing it to you."

She glanced at him. "You mean the windmill?"

Marshall felt more assured now. After all, he was twenty-six, and he was from St. Louis. "You didn't even know what a windmill was until I came along."

"I saw windmills when we were in Holland last summer, Mister Marshall."

Marshall took a deep breath. He had talked too fast. He started to explain, but he saw the glint in those blue eyes, and he kept still. Well, there were other ways to bring a woman to time. His sales manager had said: "Be aggressive. Be bold. Take the initiative."

Marshall put his arm around her slim waist just above the gun belt. She promptly pivoted and slapped him on the side of the face with her left hand. It wasn't a token slap, either. It sounded loud, and it stung.

Her eyes were blazing. "You are not in Saint

Louis, Mister Marshall. Men have been shot for such actions as that . . . and not in the ear, either."

Maybe he had misjudged her. He looked at her again, and now the proud tilt of her head made him really want to touch her—but he desisted. For a moment he stared at the knee of his suit; it was starting to get threadbare. That reminded him of the two hundred dollars he had started with. He had paid train fare to Sleepy Eye and freight on the windmill; he had put up ten dollars on the team.

At that moment she stopped the horses, handed the reins to him, and said coldly: "That's our ranch house, Mister Marshall. I think you can find the way from here."

Dick Marshall flinched from the scorn in her voice. "Thank you very much, Miss Brainerd. I . . ."

Under the direct gaze of those blue eyes, so close to his, he wavered. Joan Brainerd jumped lightly down on her side of the wagon, untied the bridle reins of the bay, and floated upward into the saddle. She leaned forward, the reins were slack for a moment, and the bay thundered away through the mesquite.

Dick Marshall, chagrined, watched her leave, riding the bay like a leaf on the wind. Then he started the team and let the horses take their time.

What he would have liked most about this time was to see the sales manager. "Those people out there have millions," the sales manager had said, "and they don't know what to do with it. All they know is cattle and horses. Now get out there and sell old Bob Brainerd, and I'll give you all of West

Texas for your territory. Show them how a high-pressure man from the city operates."

He watched Joan Brainerd ride up to the corral and turn her horse over to a cowhand. There were a lot of things out here besides cattle and land that nobody had told him about, and somehow he felt ashamed that he had given her such a bad impression at the start.

The ranch house was a big, colonial-style building three stories tall, with huge white columns on the front porch and tremendous old cottonwoods all around, in the center of a colony of smaller buildings painted red. Dick Marshall drove up to the corral, stopped the team, and stepped down onto the axle hub, only to discover that he was stiff all over.

The big bay was in the corral, his sleek back shining in the sun as he tossed a wisp of hay over his withers. Marshall felt rather small now that he was on foot. A cowboy with a bandaged forearm was lacing a piece of leather on a saddle with a rawhide thong, and Dick went up to him.

"Where could I find Mister Brainerd?" he asked.

The cowboy looked at him and pushed back his hat. "You from the city?" he asked.

"Saint Louis," said Dick.

"Selling windmills, looks like." The cowboy pulled on the thong with his good hand. "The boss doesn't really like windmills . . . especially not today."

"Why not today?" asked Marshall.

The cowboy said bleakly: "Rustlers run off twenty head of calves last night, killed one hand, and shot me in the arm."

Dick Marshall stared at the wide spot of dark red on the bandage. "I'm sorry," he said, suddenly feeling very humble.

The cowboy pointed with his good arm. "The boss is riding in over there. I'll take care of your team."

"Thanks." Marshall was relieved because he wouldn't have known what to do with the team anyway. He walked to the house and intercepted the man on horseback as he rode up to the front porch.

Mr. Brainerd looked down at him—a face with ageless lines, weather-beaten cheeks, and far-seeing blue eyes like Joan's but with sharpness and perhaps anxiety in them. The older man sat straight in the saddle, like Joan, and Dick Marshall took off his straw hat.

"Mister Brainerd," he said, "I've come from Saint Louis to demonstrate a new windmill to you." He stopped. He was supposed to keep talking, but for some reason he didn't feel like it.

Mr. Brainerd looked at him without emotion. Finally he said: "Leave your rig at the barn. I'll tell my daughter to see that you're put up for the night, and I'll talk to you after supper."

Somehow, Marshall felt impelled to be honest with this man. "Frankly," he said. "I can't pay for a night's lodging."

Brainerd looked down, and his eyes did not change. "I can see that easy enough," he said dryly, "but we don't run a hotel. Make yourself at home. Supper's at six." He leaned forward, and the horse walked away.

Marshall was alone, so he wandered back to the

barn to talk with the injured cowhand. It was a dry summer. The grass was thin, but it was the first real dry summer they'd had in sixteen years. However, it was the rustlers causing the most trouble. Last year they had gotten away with half the calf crop, and this year it might be worse. That meant that in three or four years they wouldn't have anything to drive to market.

A colored boy came for Marshall at five-thirty and showed him to his room. Marshall found a place outside to wash, and finally sat down to supper at a big table with a heavy linen cloth. There was silver and cut glass and napkins, and Dick Marshall felt less sure of himself by the minute.

Arnold Page, the foreman of the ranch, came in, and there was a commission man from Kansas City, and Tom Andrews, the owner of the Bar B Bar which, Mr. Brainerd said, "takes up all the next county." They all wore boots, of course, but they seemed at home with the linen tablecloth and the cut glass.

Joan sat quietly at the head of the table, where Dick Marshall could see her by turning his eyes slightly—but she did not look at him.

"Don't you feel well, Jo?" asked her father, whose gray hair gleamed under the light of the kerosene lamps. He looked at Marshall. "She's generally talkative," he said.

He must have seen the color rise in Marshall's face, for he glanced at Joan again and said: "Have some more biscuits, Mister Marshall, and help yourself to the peach preserves. There's eight hundred quarts in the cellar."

Marshall stayed quiet, but he managed to speak to Joan as they left the supper table. "I'm sorry about today, Miss Brainerd."

Her head was high as she swept past him. "It's quite all right, Mister Marshall."

Arnold Page, the foreman, spoke his mind as Marshall got outside. "I'm against these windmills," he said, not looking at Marshall but at Brainerd. "There'd just be more complications because we'd have to take care of them. Anyway, we don't have a dry summer but once every ten years."

Marshall started to answer with an argument, but Brainerd said mildly: "The cows might put on more weight if they had plenty of water."

Page and the commission man went off to look at some horses, and Dick Marshall stayed to talk to Brainerd and Andrews. He had a chance to impress two important men, but somehow he flubbed it. He just presented his argument as briefly as possible and left the decision up to them.

Brainerd rolled a cigarette. "These machines have to be oiled and greased, I take it."

"Yes," said Marshall, wondering what he would ever do with that windmill back in Sleepy Eye.

"And repaired, too, I guess. Takes time." He struck a match on his trouser seat and lit his cigarette. "Worst is, we don't even know if these contraptions will work out here in West Texas. You ever see 'em work, Tom?"

Andrews shook his head. "Nobody's ever set one up out here."

"Well, young fellow . . ."

Marshall's hopes dropped altogether. Even if he

should get back to town, he wouldn't have money to hire a team to go to another ranch. "How deep do you find water?" he asked suddenly.

"Twenty or twenty-five feet," said Brainerd.

"You have wind, don't you?"

"That's the one thing we always have," said Andrews.

"Well, look at it this way," Marshall said earnestly, "will a steer short on water lose twenty-five pounds in a hot summer?"

"More like a hundred and twenty-five," said Andrews.

"All right," said Marshall. "Say you run four hundred steers in three sections. One Western Zephyr windmill will water that many steers. Now, twenty-five pounds apiece is ten thousand pounds . . . and that would pay for a lot of windmills. And as a matter of fact, Mister Brainerd, these windmills hardly ever require any care. Tell you what I'll do. Have you got a well out in the pasture somewhere?"

"There's that old Spanish well up near the Caprock. Cowhands stop there to water their horses."

At least he could get rid of the windmill, thought Dick Marshall. "I'll put this windmill up and you can watch it pump water out of the ground." He got reckless. "If it doesn't look good to you, I'll give it to you."

Well, it was his windmill; he had paid for it with the last portion of money left by his mother.

Brainerd studied him over the cigarette. The sun had gone down, and a coyote yipped out on the prairie. Brainerd frowned a little and looked at his hands. They were big hands.

"I generally buy or I don't buy," he said, "but you look honest. I'll let you put it up, and, if it works, then we'll see."

Marshall knew that Brainerd felt sorry for him, and probably would buy this windmill if it would work. But he wanted to sell a dozen windmills—and he didn't like charity.

He went to bed feeling pretty low. He'd never put up a windmill. In fact, Marshall had never even seen one pump water. Maybe that sales manager had been a better salesman than Dick Marshall had realized. Well, he'd have to stay on the ranch two or three days more, and the hire of the team would be more than his deposit.

The next morning Shorty, one of the two Levi'd cowboys helping him to put up the windmill, swore when he unpacked the tail vane. "Hey, Western Zephyr! That's what the last feller was selling . . . the one that Page shot in the ear!"

Dick Marshall felt more than a little ill for a while. He realized that the sales manager had sent him into this, knowing what had happened there before.

They sank the pipe and put up the tower of four-by-fours, and nailed on the braces and the ladder and connected up the pipestem. They hoisted the crown and the wheel with lariats and a saddle horse. Marshall had a picture to work by, and it was a lucky thing—by mid-afternoon of the second day the windmill was up. Shorty took off his hat in a salute. The other cowboy hollered: "*Yippee!*" Marshall released the brake and let the tail swing into place.

The wind blew, the big wheel turned, the pump

shaft went up and down—but no water came out of the pipe. Marshall frowned. He knew there was water there; he had seen it—but what about the Western Zephyr? The truth was that he didn't know if the Western Zephyr would pump water if it was in the ocean.

He watched it for a while, but nothing happened. Shorty suggested different things, but the wheel continued to go around merrily; the pump shaft rattled up and down—but no water came out. Marshall began to worry.

The two cowhands cooked supper over a campfire, and Marshall ate ravenously but morosely, and wondered what Joan was doing, but mostly he stared at the windmill wheel, now revolving so fast in the evening breeze that it was like a blur, and wondered why it didn't pump water.

One cowboy looked toward the west. The sun was down beyond the Caprock. "Gray sky," he said, throwing on another piece of cedar to keep the coffee hot. "Wind coming up, too." He glanced at his gun belt lying across his bedroll. "Good night for rustlers, Lefty."

Yes, the wind was coming up, and the wheel was going lickety-split—but no water. Marshall got up and pulled down the brake handle and latched it. The wheel whirled away from the wind and stopped turning, and he went back to the little fire.

"Why don't you wait for these rustlers some night and arrest them?" he asked to make conversation.

Shorty was scouring the skillet with sand. "It ain't that simple. It's sort of a campaign, like." He told Marshall how a man named Jones, who owned a couple of counties up over the Caprock, had tried to buy out Brainerd, and then to freeze him out.

"Why would he especially want the Walking H?" Dick Marshall asked.

Shorty pointed southwest with the skillet. "See that V up there in the mountains? That's Slicknasty Pass, and anybody driving cattle up from the Pecos would have to come through that pass.

"I thought there was a railroad along the Pecos."

"You can't send stolen cattle by rail," Shorty explained. "Too many brand inspectors. It's better to stash 'em away and work the brands over when you have plenty of time."

Dick Marshall stared. "You mean Jones handles stolen cattle?"

Lefty said: "We figger he's the biggest moonlight rancher in Texas."

The two cowboys saddled up to look for a cow that had been bawling that afternoon.

"Keep your eyes open," Shorty said to Marshall. "There's a trail about there"—he motioned— "leads to the pass. If you see some calves headin' up that way with a couple of tough jaspers behind them, you better lay low. They're good shots."

Dick Marshall nodded. It got pretty lonely as soon as they left, and he was nervous, listening for the yells that would indicate a herd. It got dark, but the moon was full and bright, and he stood by the windmill ladder and looked up. He had to do something. He couldn't keep eating free meals at the Walking H. He looked at the wheel. The damned thing had to work.

He jammed his straw hat tightly on the back of

his head and climbed the ladder with an oilcan. He crawled up on the platform and hung onto the crown while he oiled everything thoroughly. Then he got down and swung the wheel into the wind a little until it turned. He waited hopefully for fifteen minutes, but there was still no water.

He found the hammer and picked it up. He'd heard a couple of slats rattling in the big wheel, and figured they had been loosened when the wheel was thrown out of the wagon. He fingered the hammer. He couldn't see how a loose slat could make any difference—but he didn't have any choice. He'd better nail them down.

He went back up the ladder. The platform was four feet square; the wheel was five feet in diameter and mounted so it cleared the platform by about six inches. He didn't dare stand in front of the wheel, for the wind might change, and the wheel would swing around and brush him off. The only way was to climb through the braces at the center of the wheel; then he could sit on the shaft and lean out and nail the slats, and the worst that could happen was that he might get turned upside down.

He jammed his straw hat firmly on his head, stuck the hammer handle in his belt, and buttoned his black-and-white-checked coat, for the breeze up there was cool. He climbed the ladder, leaned through the iron braces to nail down the slats, but just as he started to hammer, he heard voices and stopped. Three men rode up out of the mesquite, and Dick Marshall stayed quiet. They came up to the windmill, and one rode over to the campfire and back.

"Looks like they've all three lit out somewhere ... but they'll be back. Bedrolls are still there."

The leader was right under the windmill wheel. "Follow orders," he said. "Break out the ax and start chopping. If old man Brainerd sees this thing pump water, he'll never give up."

Marshall's eyes opened wide. The rustlers had come to cut down the windmill—*his* windmill. Then a motion caught his eye from far away, and he forgot about the windmill. Four persons were coming on horseback, and now they were two hundred yards away, downwind from the rustlers and beyond a small rise. In the deepening twilight, he was sure Joan and her father were two of the four.

Marshall saw what could happen, and it chilled him: the four would ride into an ambush, and somebody might get killed.

He took a deep breath. He leaned out and held the hammer by the tip of the handle and positioned it over the leader's head and let go. "Stick 'em up!" he bellowed, loud enough to be heard a half mile. "I've got you covered!"

The leader looked up in time to get the hammer between the eyes. He swayed in the saddle, and the other two started to raise their hands. One stood with his hands in the air, but the other one suddenly spurred his horse to the other side of the windmill tower. Then a gust of wind hit the wheel and spun it around.

Dick Marshall heard the crack of wood against wood; it sounded as if the brake had been released. The wheel caught the wind with a jerk. It swung into the wind squarely, seemed to roll backward for an instant, then began to turn. The tail vane came around with a snap, and the wheel was head-on into the wind. The wheel took off with a flying start and spun furiously.

Marshall seemed to be floating in air. In seconds he lost track of the ground and closed his eyes. It didn't make any difference anyway. All he could do was hold onto the braces and spin with the wheel. He heard a shot, and the paralyzing whine of a bullet, and felt one of the iron rods vibrate painfully in his hand—but he didn't let go. Another shot, and a wooden slat cracked in two—and Marshall was turning furiously.

Then there were a lot of shots. At one turn of the wheel, Marshall glimpsed Mr. Brainerd and the two cowboys riding up in the semidarkness at whirlwind speed, with Joan close behind them. The next time he could find the ground, the three rustlers had their hands in the air, and Shorty was jerking their guns from their holsters.

Joan was out of sight. Then the tail vane of the windmill swung, and the wheel skidded to a stop. Dick Marshall pried his fingers from the iron braces and climbed out of the wheel. His hat was still tight on his head; he wiped the sweat from his forehead and went down the ladder.

He saw Joan inside the tower. She was smiling at him. He went down the ladder and turned toward Mr. Brainerd and stepped onto the ground, and slipped. It felt like mud. He stared down. Then the sound of running water beat its way through his amazement. A stream was trickling from the windmill.

Dick Marshall began to grin. "Turn it on!" he shouted.

Joan released the brake. The windmill wheel spun, the pump shaft rattled up and down, and water poured out in a two-inch stream.

"I'll be hornswoggled!" said Marshall. "It wouldn't do that this afternoon!"

Mr. Brainerd looked back.

Joan said matter-of-factly: "I saw one at Kansas City, and the man said the leathers had to be soaked up before it would pump."

Mr. Brainerd got off his horse and looked at the water coming from the windmill. "Well, I guess it works," he said.

Dick Marshall said proudly: "It's a Western Zephyr . . . it *has* to work."

Mr. Brainerd looked at him suspiciously but said nothing. *Too bad*, thought Marshall, *you don't know a good windmill when you see one*.

The best thing was that Marshall rode back to the ranch behind Joan's saddle, and it was necessary—especially as he had never ridden a horse before—to put his arms around her waist occasionally. She did not seem to object, since it was strictly in the line of duty.

The rustlers looked tough but not very mean with their hands in the air. They dismounted in front of the big house, and Mr. Brainerd turned to Marshall. "You helped us capture those gunhands, and one is talking already. You ought to have a reward."

Marshall said stiffly: "I didn't do it for you. They were about to cut down my windmill."

The moon was higher, and Mr. Brainerd looked at it and then at Marshall. "*Your* windmill?" he asked.

Dick Marshall said: "They wouldn't trust us with that much credit."

"What's your commission on one windmill?" asked Mr. Brainerd.

"I make fifty dollars a sale," Marshall said.

"I'll take the one you put up," said Mr. Brainerd, "and order me a couple of dozen more. You can make out the order tomorrow morning."

Marshall gulped and looked at Joan. She was smiling. Her hair looked black in the moonlight. Marshall turned back to Mr. Brainerd, but the rancher had disappeared. Dick Marshall turned again to Joan. "I wasn't really looking for that," he said, not too sure of his breath.

She smiled up at him. "You may not have heard," she said, "that Westerners are people of action."

Well, yes, he had sort of heard that, and he didn't want to seem out of place, so he kissed her on the mouth, and she didn't seem to mind. In fact, she helped.

# Tough *Hombre*

When Big Blue Buckley was pushing steel through the mountains of Colorado Territory in the 'Seventies, he had only one policy: "It takes guts to build a railroad." So when they wanted a man to lay track through Sonora in the Republic of Mexico in 1880, they said: "It takes Buckley to build a railroad."

They found him in a high mountain pass, driving spikes with his crew in ten below zero weather against a forty-mile blizzard from the northwest. They got him into his foreman's shack over a pot of hot coffee and told him: "If we can get three hundred miles of track from Guaymas, Mexico, to Nogales, Arizona, by the end of Eighteen Eighty-Two, Porfirio Díaz will give us ten thousand dollars a mile. It's wild country, and maybe materials will be scarce. Think you can do it?"

Buckley looked through the tiny window at the snow streaming by outside. He could see a flatcar loaded with rails sitting on the length of track he had just spiked. The snow was filling up the spaces among the loaded rails. He turned back to the officials. His pale blue eyes lighted up with the only kind of exultation he ever showed.

"I can build a railroad anywhere," he said. "With anything."

So they sent him down to Guaymas on the Golfo de Cortés, with the pick of his Kansas-toughened crews, to build a grade and spike rails through a desert infested with cacti, rattlesnakes, outlaws, and buzzards. Big Blue didn't hesitate. Maybe he didn't know Sonora was outside of the United States. Maybe he didn't care.

He started asking for more help while the engineers were still hammering down a wharf on Ardilla Island out in the bay and even before they started throwing a trestlework across a thousand feet of shallow water to the mainland. Help was slow in coming. They told Buckley it was hard to get reliable men to go to Mexico. Buckley sent back a characteristic answer: "I didn't ask for reliable men. Just get me somebody who can handle a span of mules or is willing to learn. Get 'em out of the penitentiaries . . . anywhere. But get 'em fast."

He was already running grade toward Hermosillo, but it was too slow to suit him. He had a hundred Yaqui Indians on the picks and shovels, but the Yaquis were cousins of the Apaches; they were fighters by heritage and not laborers, and Big Blue found out he couldn't push them. When he bellowed at them, they stared back inscrutably and went on taking their time.

Then one blistering hot day in October a windjammer sailed up the Gulf from a three-month journey around the Horn, and half a hundred men disembarked. Big Blue was waiting for them at the railroad camp north of Guaymas. He was standing on top of the fresh grade. He was built like the trunk of an oak, and his skin had the look of well-tanned leather. His eyes took in the men getting out of the wagons and began to narrow. He strode back to meet them.

The first man was six feet one and lean but not thin; his sloping shoulders indicated strength. His dark face, much too sharply lined for a young man, indicated something Buckley didn't like.

"What's your name?" asked Buckley, stopping.

"Wade Gholson," said the tall man belligerently.

"Where you from?"

"East."

Buckley looked over the others. "Are you all together?"

"All together," said Gholson. "All that's left of us. One man got his throat cut when we were off Brazil. Another fell overboard off Lima. There's only forty-five left."

Buckley plowed down the loose side of the grade and stopped in front of Gholson. "Are you looking for work or for trouble?"

By that time the forty-four other newcomers were ranged alongside Gholson and back of him, but Buckley did not appear to notice. The Mexican Yaquis on the other side of the grade stopped work to watch.

Gholson said insolently: "I'm not afraid of trouble. I killed a man up in Maine with a spike maul. That's one reason I left the States."

"What's the other reason?" asked Buckley.

"The other reason is about my brother."

"Who's your brother?"

"My brother was Vince Gholson," he said slowly. "You killed him with a spike maul up in Indian Territory a couple of years back."

The hot desert air whistled in through Buckley's nostrils. He nodded as if to himself. "He looked like you," he said. "I knew there was something . . ." He glanced at the men back of Gholson, at the men alongside. "You've had three months to tell these fellows all about it, haven't you?"

"I told them," said Gholson flatly. "And they're with me."

Buckley seemed to make up his mind suddenly. His face swelled, and a blue tint crept over his mahogany skin. Gholson must have known what was coming, but he didn't do something about it fast enough. Buckley's big fist flashed, and Gholson's head shot back with a crack of neck bones. He stumbled and fell. He got to his feet, swinging. Buckley went after him into the middle of the crowd. He hit Gholson again, and Gholson fell again.

Gholson got up swaying, with murder in his eyes. He came forward drawing a knife. Buckley's big fist exploded on his jaw. Gholson went down. Then Big Blue jerked him to his feet by the collar of his lumberjack shirt. Buckley's fury was gone. "All I'm interested in," he said, "is can you skin a span of mules? Draw yourself a team of jugheads and see if this hundred and ten degree sun will boil some of the trouble out of you."

Buckley didn't even take the man's knife. He spun him around and shoved him hard. Gholson's feet got tangled, and he went down on his face in the alkali dirt. Buckley turned to the others. "There's work to do," he said. He waved a big arm, and they scattered. Gholson was getting up. Buckley's back was toward him. Buckley climbed the grade and walked away.

He met a pair of mules pulling a dump bucket and driven by a tough, little Irishman wearing black work clothes that were grimed with white sweat salt. The Irishman said out of the corner of his mouth: "You should've hit him harder. You only made him mad."

Big Blue Buckley snorted. "He can't drive mules if he's layin' up somewhere with a broken neck."

O'Connell muttered: "I've seen some tough gangs on the U.P., but this bunch off the boat is the cut-throatingest bunch I ever laid eyes on. They must have scoured all the toughest dives in China for 'em."

Buckley grinned at him. "Every last one of them is running from the law," he said. "You can see it in their faces. They took jobs to get out of the country. They figure they'll raise a lot of hell, and I'll fire them, then nobody will go looking for them. But they're going to get a surprise," he said pleasantly. "They're going to learn how to build railroads."

Five hundred graders were working toward Hermosillo, ninety miles north of Guaymas. They grubbed out mesquite roots; they filled in cuts, scraped down rises, laid culverts, built up the grade, and topped it with rock ballast. The route was mostly over desert, but behind them, back toward Guaymas, the powder men were blasting a cut through the foothills of the western range of the Sierra Madres, and ahead of them, near Hermosillo, the engineers and steel men were throwing a bridge over the Río Sonora.

That first afternoon Wade Gholson sullenly followed a drag bucket behind a span of big Missouri mules. He had the reins over his shoulder. He tipped the bucket to scoop up a load of frosty-looking alkali dirt. He cracked his whip over the mules' backs, and followed them at a half run as the bucket slid free. His feet sank ankle-deep in the loose dirt, and curtains of dust hung in the heat of the sun.

His mules came to the fill. He heaved on the big handle with both hands to dump the load. But he didn't turn loose fast enough. He was thrown over the bucket onto the heels of the mules. He was kicked in the ribs, but he rolled out of the way of the overturned bucket. When he got to his feet, he glared maliciously at Buckley. He still had the whip in one hand, and he fingered it.

Buckley's eyes stayed flat and deadly. He knew what Gholson was thinking. The man wanted to wrap that blacksnake around his neck. But Buckley wasn't ready for a showdown. He had nipped off the first show of trouble; now he would let it grow a little under Gholson's leadership. Gholson had made an indirect threat about a spike maul. Presently Buckley would give him a chance to prove up on it.

The next three weeks went fast. Two hundred Mexicans under big straw hats worked leisurely but ceaselessly with pick and shovel to level an alkali hill, while the drivers dragged the loosened dirt away and filled it into a gully. Sun-parched men cursed the mules, lashed them with black-snakes, tied red-figured handkerchiefs over their own noses, and followed the dump buckets, while other crews beyond the gully were scraping and grading, and loggers were up in the hills, cutting ties from the hard, dense wood of fustic trees.

Buckley strode up and down the grade, goading the Mexicans, swearing at the graders. His big body could be seen somewhere on the grade at any hour of the day. In those three weeks he did not fight. Gholson and his crowd hung together. They became more sullen, more uncooperative, but they avoided a break with him. That suited Buckley; he would give them an excuse to fight soon enough. One of them was killed by another over a card game in the middle of the night, but Buckley did not interfere, although O'Connell and the other veterans of the Union Pacific track crews looked at him questioningly.

"As long as they kill their own crowd," said Buckley indifferently, "it's none of my business."

Buckley seemed intent on one thing only: to push the grade to the Sonora River by the time the bridge gang got through there. It was almost as though the grade were a physical extension of himself, and he would will it to be extended a certain number of miles every day.

He knew that Gholson would try to kill him. He could see it in the man's rebellious eyes, in the set of his jaw. He sensed it in the attitude of the forty or more men around the coffeepot fire the night they were waiting for the supper call, and he strode into the middle of the group and said: "Work tonight."

Nobody answered. Buckley looked at Gholson. Gholson took a deep breath, but he didn't get up; he leaned down and began to untie the rawhide laces of his shoe.

"From now on," said Buckley, "there'll be plenty of night work. That's why you're getting two and a quarter a day."

From the corner of his eye he saw Gholson hold up his shoe and drain the sand out of it. He left. Up at the cook wagon, O'Connell was leaving with a plate of antelope steak and biscuits and a big tin cup of coffee. He said to Buckley: "Is that bunch going to work with us tonight?"

Buckley glared at him. "If I hadn't known you since Eighteen Sixty-Seven," he said, "I'd knock you over the cook wagon."

But it was a shock to him when O'Connell said: "You'd better save your strength."

O'Connell went on, found his spot in the sand, crossed his feet, and dropped back, holding his food far out to balance. Buckley took a big breath. So the Irish terriers were getting restless for a showdown. It had better come soon, then.

It came the next day. A message arrived from the engineer at Guaymas. Buckley read it and smiled with satisfaction. And that night he chose a moment when Gholson was at the cook wagon, getting his grub. Buckley stood with his back to the wagon, legs apart like leaning tree trunks, and bellowed: "I want eight spikers for tomorrow morning. We start laying track at Guaymas." He half turned. "O'Connell, you drove spikes on the K.P."

O'Connell, his mouth full, nodded. Buckley

looked at Gholson. "I heard you can handle a spike maul," Buckley said.

He saw the light rise in the man's dark eyes, and he knew that was what Gholson had been waiting for. Gholson nodded. "I'll drive with you," he said pointedly.

Buckley passed on. He asked for more, and counted off seven spikers and four helpers. Then he looked at Gholson and grinned, his sun-whitened lips forming a square. "I'll take a hand for a few days," he said. "I'm out of practice."

They worked until ten o'clock that night. Then the sun went down west of the opal-tinted hills. The daylight was gone suddenly. The Mexicans dropped their picks and shovels and began to walk back along the grade.

Buckley came striding after them. "You!" he yelled hoarsely. "Where you going? Where's the mayor? Diego!"

A fat Mexican with an enormous straw hat and a dusty blanket over his shoulder walked out of the group. "*Si, señor,*" he said placatingly.

"Get your men back on the job!"

Diego temporized. "Boss, the sun . . . she's gone. We work no more today."

Buckley roared: "You're getting paid for it, aren't you?"

"We go home now to our *niños*. We come back tomorrow morning . . . *mañana*."

Buckley exploded. "*Mañana*, hell! We've got a railroad to build. You grab that pick and start digging . . . now! *¡Pronto!*"

Diego turned to his countrymen. They talked in

excited Spanish, with many gesticulations. Then Diego turned back to Buckley. "We no work tonight," he explained patiently. "We go . . ."

Buckley hit him. They heard the smack of hard bone against the Mexican's face. Then he yelled: "Get back to work, you sons-of-seacooks! ¡*Andale!*"

They went slowly, muttering. Two of them helped Diego to his feet.

Gholson said plainly: "He can bat the Mexicans around easy enough."

Buckley looked at O'Connell and saw the same feeling expressed in O'Connell's face. Buckley sighed and began to stretch his great shoulders.

They were up the next morning before daylight. At four o'clock, thirteen of them got into a spring wagon pulled by a span of mules. Buckley gave a last-minute order to his *segundo:* "Get that grade north!" He got a small bottle of mescal from the timekeeper's shack, and they set off for Guaymas.

It was afternoon when they pulled in. Buckley had killed the mescal and thrown away the bottle, while Gholson watched him with sardonic eyes.

In Guaymas a few scrawny chickens were picking up weed seeds, and small razor-backed pigs ran in between the adobe huts when the spring wagon's wheels cut through the fetlock-deep dust. There was scurrying and muttered—"*Gringos!*"— as the wagon went through the town and down to the water.

The trestlework from the island was finished. It had no solid floor but was laid with ties and ready for rails. Buckley led the twelve men. They walked the ties to the island, where a windjammer was unloading rails with a steam winch.

A gang of Mexicans was at the dock, and Buckley organized them, five pairs of men to a rail. They set the first pair of rails on the ties, and Buckley lined them up. Two men went in and set the spikes. Then Buckley waved his big arm at the spike maulers.

They nailed it down—all but Gholson, who was impaired. He stood easily, leaning on the handle of the big steel maul. Buckley had the Mexicans bring up the second pair of rails, while he stood at the far end and sighted down the steel and straightened it. Then he handed the width gauge to one of the helpers. "Keep 'em going," he said. "I'll spike."

He expanded his big chest and looked at Gholson. Gholson looked back. Gholson's expression did not change. There was satisfaction in it. This was to his liking.

Buckley's pale blue eyes were flat and hard. He spat on his hands, hefted a spike maul, and stepped into place. He faced forward, and that left Gholson to face backward. They took alternate blows. Buckley swung fast, and Gholson had to watch to keep in time. Gholson was swinging right-handed. Buckley hardly changed his position over the rail. He swung right-handed on the outside and left-handed on the inside. He took the first swing, and he didn't miss. It was always a good solid blow, and no spikes shot out from under the head of his heavy maul.

Steel went out on the trestle, and within an hour there was a flatcar on the rails alongside the ship.

They piled rails on the flatcar, and a dozen Mexicans rolled it out on the bridge to the spiking gang. The began to spike in earnest, for the flatcar was always just behind them, and the Mexicans did not have to carry rails all the way from the ship.

The sweat began to pour out of Buckley, and it seemed to loosen his muscles. It didn't sober him, for his voice was thick as he roared at the Mexicans: "*¡Andale! ¡Andale!*" But the pace of his spiking did not ease; he swung, it seemed, ever harder and always faster.

Energies were drained by the blazing sun; empty stomachs were painful, but always there was the iron head of Buckley's maul, rising and falling, rising and falling, with the dull clank of maul heads against iron spikes, and Buckley's hoarse—"*¡Andale!*"— which kept the Mexicans running forward, dropping rail after rail with crashes that shivered the trestle.

Gholson kept driving. He watched his aim. There was power in his long, solid blows and satisfaction on his dark face as he watched Buckley's thick neck grow redder and redder.

By six o'clock they were three-fourths of the way to the shore at Guaymas, and two Mexicans came from shore, picking their way across the ties, each carrying a big bucket in each hand. One of the Mexicans was the big-stomached Diego.

O'Connell and his spiking partner, at the end of the rail, laid down their mauls and went to meet the Mexicans. Gholson backed up two ties and finished driving the next spike with Buckley. O'Connell was biting ravenously into a sandwich made

of great slabs of heavy white bread and thick slices
of burro meat.

Gholson started to lay down his maul, but a blast
from Buckley froze him. "Where you going?"

He looked up. Buckley was glaring at him. Gholson took a deep breath, and his face showed that he
was ready. He straightened up slowly, still holding
the handle of his spike maul. The two Mexicans
went past them. Gholson said: "I'm going to eat."

Buckley roared: "There's another spike to drive!"

Gholson spat out the words contemptuously:
"Drive it."

Buckley began to swell up. He said ominously:
"Pick up that spike maul and drive that spike or
defend yourself."

Big Diego was standing just behind Buckley.
Diego's white teeth were showing.

"Come on, you tough guy!" Buckley roared.
"What are you waiting on?"

Gholson recovered his spike maul in one smooth
motion that seemed to suck it up into his hands.
He stepped forward onto the next tie and swung
the heavy iron head in an arc that would have
crushed Buckley's head.

Buckley stepped back heavily. He brought up his
hammer and lashed out with the maul before
Gholson had stopped his own.

Gholson sucked in his stomach as the iron maul
head whistled by. It grazed his belt buckle. He
stepped back, feeling with his foot for the tie behind him. Buckley roared and followed.

Gholson was off balance for a moment. He
dodged the next swing, but the maul caught him

hard in the ribs. They cracked. He swung his maul backhanded and the handle caught Buckley across the forearm.

Buckley crowded him, stalked him along the ties, his face blue, his breath coming in stentorous grunts. The men on the spiking crew backed away with watchful eyes, saying nothing. Diego still stood back next to the flatcar, watching.

The sweat squeezed out on Gholson's forehead. He swung the maul again and again, but it seemed to be getting heavy. He put a solid blow on Buckley's thigh, but the man didn't even wince.

He stepped away and smashed Buckley's shoulder. Buckley grunted, and his left arm fell limp, but he swung the maul with his big right arm as if it didn't make any difference. Gholson barely had time to meet the maul head with his own. The steel clanged, and the heads rebounded sharply.

Buckley recovered first. His hand slid up the handle of the maul to shorten his grip. He swung at Gholson's neck. Gholson dodged back, and then tried to counter, but this time there was no strength in his blow. He was breathing harshly and unevenly.

Buckley's big arm was swinging the maul in an eight-foot circle. It whistled once around his head and went at Gholson's face. Gholson was moving back, Buckley after him. Gholson stepped on the handle of O'Connell's maul and stumbled. Buckley's maul went past his cheekbones.

Gholson was down on the ties. He straightened with a surge of desperation and threw his maul at Buckley's face. Buckley ducked, and the maul went over his head, described a long arc, and splashed into the water. Buckley stood there, waiting for him to get up. His maul was cocked over his shoulder. He said: "Come on up, tough guy! If you're not whipped . . . you're sitting on a spike maul."

Gholson took a deep breath. His sweaty face held a look of dazed surprise. He got up empty-handed. Buckley glared at him and said more quietly: "You find what you were looking for when you came out here?"

Gholson stood there on the ties and looked at Big Blue. Gholson's words came with difficulty, from hot and laboring lungs. "I'll drive that other spike," he said.

Buckley's pale blue eyes showed nothing. His face was expressionless. He waited, watching, as Gholson picked up O'Connell's maul. They drove the spike. Buckley watched Gholson as the man laid down the maul. Then Buckley said: "If you want to know about your brother, I'll tell you. Or ask O'Connell, or anybody who saw it."

Gholson stood up straight for a second. His face was white from exhaustion. He said: "I reckon Vince asked for it. That was a habit of his." Gholson's eyes were inscrutable as he added: "I reckon you gave him the same chance that you gave me."

He turned and went slowly toward the buckets of food, while Diego, standing behind Buckley, showed his teeth in a grin.

"It take a veree tough *hombre*," he remarked, "to build a railroad."

# The Stick and the
# Bearded Lady

Mose Grumstrup, bald-headed except for a fringe of grizzly gray hair but wearing a glossy black beard, looked quite patriarchal until you got to his eyes. They were small and sharp. He stood in the open end of the midway—for this was in the day when few carnivals dared charge admission, especially in a small town—and glanced suspiciously at the sun, which was about to sink behind the Hungry Horse Mountains, and then back at the rodeo in the open pasture across the street.

He fingered the five gold double eagles in the pocket of his flowered waistcoat. "I hope," he grumbled to his stick, "those bronc'-busters don't all get killed off." And he added from the wisdom of sharp experience: "I can still take five hundred out of this town . . . if nothing happens."

His stick—the come-on man—was a small person whose chief characteristic was his complete mousy nonentity. He swallowed and said meekly: "It must take a lot of nerve to ride a bucking horse."

In the open pasture before a standing crowd, a man in a big droopy hat was earing down a horse. A second cowboy swung up into the saddle. The man holding the ears jumped back and the broncho erupted. The rider had his hat in his right hand. He slapped it across the horse's rump and let out a long, wild yell. Sudden gunshots sounded, and puffs of black smoke drifted from six-shooters held skyward.

Mose jumped at the shots. "I hate Texas towns," he said vehemently. "A man can't turn an honest dollar without the risk of getting hardware in his ribs."

The stick looked at him and said: "Westerners gamble on anything, though. I guess that's why they bet on your wheel . . . or Two-Fingered Halvorson's," he added hastily, for Mose glared at him.

"They're cheap sports," Mose pronounced sourly. "They hung Slick Simpson to an oak tree up near Amarillo when a couple of cowboys found out he had a gaff on the wheel." Mose swallowed nervously. "That was two weeks ago . . . just before you showed up," he remembered, and for the first time he looked at the mousy little man.

The stick said sadly: "When I still had my twelve hundred dollars." He was thoughtful for a moment, and went on: "When do you suppose that federal man will bring back my money?" His voice was mildly plaintive. "I want to get back in the sandwich stand. I don't like taking money away from cowboys on a roulette wheel."

"What's the matter with that?" Mose demanded.

The stick said, watching Mose cautiously: "They risk their lives, and they're lucky if they make three hundred dollars a season. Most of that they spend on feed for their horses. Half of them never have a decent meal themselves."

"They get entertainment on my wheel, don't they?" Mose demanded.

"I know you keep telling me it's all the same . . . somebody else will get it if you don't. But," the stick persisted, "it doesn't seem exactly right. I'd rather be back in the sandwich business . . . if I could get a stake." He looked at Mose wishfully.

Mose changed the subject. "I'm protecting you, ain't I? Didn't I step in and tell the federal man I'd be responsible for you?" He looked away and said casually: "I still can't figure out where you got all that counterfeit money."

The stick looked up the midway to the freak show. His eyes stopped at the picture of the bearded lady. He still thought she looked good and sweet and kind, and he didn't think the whiskers were real. She wasn't as young as the spider girl who had joined up a few days after the stick, but she had liked the stick's sandwiches, and not many people ever noticed him at all. He knew Mose Grumstrup spent a lot of time around her, but he didn't think she cared too much for a sharper like Mose, who didn't even have a wheel then. In fact, he didn't have any connection with the carnival except that he just went along with it, and hung around the bearded lady.

A few days after the stick had opened, the bearded lady had given him a big roll of bills and asked him to keep it with his money, because, she whispered: "You're one of the few men I can trust." The stick remembered Mose's eyes, and he thought he knew what she meant, so he put her roll with his and put a rubber band around the two rolls to hold them together.

That night the federal man came. He claimed he was looking for phony money, but he didn't find any until he got to the stick. He examined the two rolls, and the first bill on the outside of the bearded lady's roll he said was counterfeit, and he would have to take both rolls to New Orleans for examination.

He was a good-looking man with a rather high voice. He scribbled out a receipt and told the stick he would let him know. Then he seemed to consider taking the stick along with him, but Mose stepped in and said he would vouch for the stick.

The stick had been very grateful. Of course, he was flat broke, and he had to sell his sandwich stand to Two-Finger Halvorson for five dollars to get some eating money, but Mose Grumstrup started up a frame the next day with a roulette wheel that he bought from Two-Finger, and he offered the stick a job.

That was when the stick had become a stick. From the very first he didn't care for the job of fooling cowboys into betting on a gaffed wheel, but Mose explained that it was quite customary, and, anyway, Mose had vouched for him, so he couldn't run away from the carnival and leave Mose holding the sack, any more than he could tell who was the real owner of the counterfeit bills.

No, he thought sadly, he'd much rather make sandwiches—big, juicy slabs of beef, dripping with dill pickle juice, between thick slices of bread—and he could make good bread, too. Everybody liked his sandwiches, and he never had to call for help to slough the joint because he'd taken a month's wages away from somebody on a phony ... on a wheel. He liked to sell sandwiches and give people their money's worth. He'd joined up with the carnival at Sweetwater because the grease-joint man had gotten shot in an argument over short change, and they had told the stick he could make some good money. Which he had—until the night the federal man came in and took his roll.

Everybody had acted surprised—but the stick hadn't told where he'd gotten the counterfeit money, any more than he was telling now. He looked up at Mose. There was a lady involved in this, and you couldn't let a lady take a rap like that. He wasn't sure Mose would understand. He said: "Do you think the bearded lady's whiskers are real?"

Mose glared at him. Then he straightened his black broadcloth coat with the velvet collar and long tails. He lifted his tall beaver hat that was bigger at the top, settled it firmly on his head, and said: "The Man is starting the engine. The lights will be on in a minute, and the rodeo crowd is breaking up. Let's get set. And don't forget ... your cut is twenty percent of all I make on the chumps you help me with."

They went across the runway. They reached the frame. Mose lifted a canvas flap at one end, and went in. He stood up behind a narrow counter that held the roulette wheel. Behind him on a moth-eaten red velvet cloth was the flash—dolls, plaster cats, felt banners that said CALIFORNIA OR BUST and REMEMBER THE ALAMO, shaving mugs, and four thick, woolly, imported Scotch blankets that had been bought and sold back and forth in the carnival now for nearly six years. At least, that was what Two-Finger had told the stick.

The rodeo crowd was streaming across the open space and into the runway down the right side. The men from twenty-one to thirty years old headed a little furtively for the girl show, and Mose said to the stick, who was leaning against the counter at one end: "The Man is letting the girls show their navels tonight. That's a good sign. The fix is in, and we can shoot the limit."

The little kids headed for the merry-go-'round. The family groups—dignified father, worried mother, and from three to six children dressed up in their Sunday clothes, all starched and stiff—stopped at the educational exhibits—the freak show and the mechanical farm.

The midway began to warm up. The spielers went into their ballies, the hula girls paraded on the narrow platform in front of their tent, the minstrel show was putting on a teaser, the lone grab-joint man was bawling—"Get your nice, hot, juicy sandwiches here!"—and doing a thumping business, although he didn't put in half as much meat as the stick had used. The spider girl was drawing a small but dependable crowd of young Hoosiers who would say wisely that it was done with a mirror and would flip up dimes to catch the reflection and prove it.

The engine was chugging now. The arc lights came on. Mose pulled his tall hat down tightly on his bald head and rubbed his hands. He motioned his stick to watch close. There'd be a Hoosier along any minute. The noise was deafening, and that was a good sign. The dust was rising but not just in the middle. The only thing that seemed to bother Mose Grumstrup was the occasional crash of a six-shooter fired into the sky. On those occasions, the stick noted, Mose's long fingers would grip the edge of the counter, and his knuckles would turn white.

Two-Finger Halvorson, on the right, had a chump—a nice-looking young man trying to impress his girl, the stick thought, feeling sorry for him. The young man was laboring under the delusion that he might win one of Two-Finger's blankets, and Mose snorted. "Anybody can tell by looking at Two-Finger that he isn't giving away anything on that phony upright wheel," he told the stick.

Broadway Jones, on the left, had a chump, too. Then they spotted a lone cowboy coming around the bend. The cowboy was tall and wore an enormous black hat with a brim six inches wide. He looked awkward in high-heeled boots, but he walked with the bowlegged litheness of a full-grown panther. He wore a gun belt studded with cartridges and a holster that hung low on his thigh and bulged with an enormous six-shooter.

The stick looked at Mose. Mose was sizing up the cowboy, and the stick felt a little sad, because he knew the answer. The cowboy was a lone lamb and probably had a wad of C-notes from the rodeo and was looking for a place to invest them. The stick sighed. It didn't seem right. And he, the stick, would be called on to help Mose with the shearing, and he'd have to help because Mose had saved him from going to Leavenworth.

Mose threw back his head a little and began to sing: "Come one, come all. Spend a nickel, make a dollar. Spend a dollar, make a twenty."

The stick was already walking away. He went over to Broadway Jones's frame, ducked behind it, went through the dark to Two-Finger's frame, and then sauntered back to Mose's frame just ahead of the big cowboy. Mose kept singing as if he'd never seen the stick in his life. The stick stopped, looked at the wheel, pretended to consider, then threw down a nickel without a word.

Mose spun the wheel. It had hardly stopped when he sang out: "You win a dollar, mister. Take your money or let it lay."

The stick nodded without looking up. Mose spun the wheel. The big cowboy came closer and stopped. "You win a five-dollar bill," Mose announced loudly to the stick. "Take your money or let it lay." He strung out five iron dollars as he talked, making them clank solidly.

The stick reached as if undecided. "It's your money," sang Mose. "You can take it or let it lay. Leave a two and win a twenty."

The stick picked up three of the iron dollars. The cowboy was watching. Mose spun the wheel, and the pointer stopped on a red space. Mose sang out: "You win a twenty." He sounded disgusted. The cowboy edged closer. Mose threw down a big gold coin and flipped his thumb at the stick. The stick picked up the coin and backed away, shaking his head as if he couldn't understand it.

"Step up and try your luck, mister," sang Mose to the cowboy. "Play a dollar. Win a twenty."

The cowboy walked into the light. He was *big*— but his money was as good as the next chump's. Mose said: "Put up a dollar, mister. I spin the arrow. If the pointer stops anywhere on a red mark, you win twenty."

The big cowboy seemed to be fascinated by the wheel, but he shook his head.

"I'll up the odds," said Mose. He dropped a dozen pieces of red cardboard at intervals around the wheel. His hands moved fast. He laid the cards down between the nails so as to increase the red spaces all over the wheel except for a forty-five-degree portion under his left elbow. "Put up one and win a twenty," he said.

The cowboy shook his head, but the stick, watching from the side, saw he wasn't too firm. Mose saw it, too, and a sharp little gleam of victory came in his eyes.

"Maybe you're not a gambling man," said Mose with an adroit change of tactics. "Then just play for fun, mister. Play anything. Play a nickel. A lonesome nickel, mister. Play a nickel and win a quarter."

The cowboy did not move closer, but he seemed to ponder. Then a nickel dribbled out onto the counter. Mose spun the wheel and let it run free. "What's your angle, mister?" he asked.

"Huh?"

"What do you do?"

The big cowboy was watching the wheel die. "I won the bronc'-riding this afternoon," he said.

Mose stiffened for an instant. The stick knew what he was thinking. This chump had anyway two or three Cs—maybe six or eight, if he had any money to bet on himself.

Mose let him win a quarter. The stick stood at one side, fingering the twenty-dollar gold piece. "Now," said Mose, obviously annoyed at this chump who was so slow on the uptake, "play your quarter and win a dollar. You can't lose, mister."

The cowboy nodded. He was still standing too far away. Mose liked for them to crowd the counter. Then they were ripe. Mose spun the wheel. The pointer stopped on red. "You win," he announced, shaking his head as if perplexed. "It's your dollar. Take it away. Or wait. Maybe you want to see some action that's more your size, mister. Big Western cowboy with boots and spurs and chaps and six-shooter." He almost winced when he mentioned six-shooter, but went on bravely: "Tell you what I'll do. Play your dollar. You've only got a nickel in it, anyway. Play your dollar and win a five. Win a five or your choice of any blanket in the booth. Whatta you say, cowboy?"

The cowboy shook his head and kept the dollar in his hand. He seemed to be laboring under some restraint, but the stick didn't get the angle. The cowboy began to back away, slowly.

"Look," said Mose desperately, "business is crummy in Mondovi. I thought this was a town with a lot of sports," he complained, "but I guess I was wrong. Let's you and me just have some fun.

No gambling. Just play for the fun of it. Play your dollar. You've only got a nickel in it. Put up one dollar of your own. Bet my own money against me and win ten." He turned back, muttering as if to himself: "We'll get some action around here, if I have to pay for it myself. Here." His hands flashed. He sprinkled more red cards until half of the spaces on the wheel were red—all except that eighth of a circle under his left arm. "There. What do you say to that? Let's you and me have a little private game here. We won't make any money, but we'll have some fun."

He was watching the cowboy from the corner of his eye, and he saw the cowboy still wasn't sold. He glanced at the stick. The stick stepped up by the cowboy. "I'll play the dollar for you," the stick told the cowboy in a low voice. "I just made twenty. I can afford it. Here." He threw out a gold coin, bigger than a silver dollar. It vibrated on the counter for a second. The cowboy watched it, and his eyes began to flicker.

Mose rubbed his hands. "A double goose!" he sang out. "The man plays one out of the double goose. One dollar on the wheel of fortune. 'Round and 'round the little wheel goes, and where she stops nobody knows." Which was not strictly true, and never would be unless Mose should break the leg that operated the gaff.

The pointer stopped on a red mark, and Mose jumped as if he had been shot. "The big boy from Texas wins a ten on the one he didn't put up. Easy work, my friend, easy money." He was singing loud so Two-Finger could see that he had a mark.

He might need to use Two-Finger for a bank if the mark had plenty of money.

A little fever came in the cowboy's eyes. The stick saw Mose relax and knew it was all over but the kill. Mose settled his big hat down tightly on his head and drew in a deep breath for his next song.

Then it happened. Mose held his breath. A girl, dark-haired, slim, lithe, and warm-eyed, popped out of the milling crowd on the midway and came running over to the big cowboy and fastened herself to his arm, with her big wide eyes looking up into his, and then the stick knew the angle.

"What are you doing, Jim?" she asked fearfully.

The big cowboy looked down at her, and the stick felt sick, for the cowboy's expression took on truculence, and the stick recognized a familiar sight: the man didn't like to be restrained by his wife, especially in front of others, because it made him feel childish. Mose let out his breath again. Mose, too, was a student of human nature, and those little things didn't get by him.

"I just been watching the wheel go 'round, Mary," the big cowboy said, half defiantly.

She looked at the gold pieces on the counter, and a flash of concern came over her face. "Jim," she said anxiously, "you aren't gambling?"

Jim said belligerently: "I've only got a nickel of my money in there."

"Jim," she said earnestly, "we need that bronc'-riding money. I don't want to take the children through another winter without flour."

Mose spoke up to help out the cowboy. "Look, madam," he said, "your husband has just won ten dollars of my money without putting up a nickel. The nickel he put up is in that dollar in his hand. The ten he just won was on a dollar put up by this kind gentleman here." Mose jerked his thumb at the stick without taking his eyes from the girl. "You wouldn't begrudge me a chance to at least win my money back, would you, madam? I have to make a living, too, and my children get hungry the same as yours." That wasn't true, either, as far as the stick knew, for if Mose had a family, he'd never told anybody about it, and certainly the bearded lady wouldn't have encouraged Mose if she had thought he was married. "Tell you what I'll do," said Mose. "There's a ten there. Let the ten lay, and I'll put up just one dollar of your own. Ten will get you sixty if you win. If you don't win, I get my money back. If you do win, you've got seventy. What do you say, madam? Is that fair enough?"

"Well," she said doubtfully, "if he isn't any betting any of his own money . . ."

The cowboy threw down the dollar in his hand, and Mose spun the wheel. He looked at the stick and nodded twice, then once more, toward Two-Finger's frame. The stick moved slowly. It looked as if Mose would make a killing.

The stick moved back. The pointer had stopped on red. Mose scowled his best scowl, then laid down four gold pieces; they clanked on each other. "It isn't my night," he moaned. "I can't win for losing. What's gone wrong with my luck?"

"Take it, Jim," the girl said quickly. "Take it and let's go."

But Mose was starting his pitch again. "I've still got ten in that great big beautiful goose," he said.

"I can't change a twenty. It's bad luck to break a twenty. And you've got seventy-one dollars there on the board. You're a lucky man. It's your lucky night, and your lucky girl is beside you. Now, I'll tell you what I'll do. That seventy-one will get you a hundred and fifty you can't do it again. What do you say? You can't lose. You haven't got a nickel of your own money on the counter, mister. You're betting against me with my own money. Put up five of your own just to show your good faith. What do you say? Seventy-six gets you a hundred and fifty. You can't lose because you aren't even betting with your own money."

The big cowboy was fascinated by now. He wasn't watching the wheel. He was watching the gold. The girl's eyes were big. She was watching the gold, too. The cowboy dropped a quarter eagle on the board.

The stick sighed. He went on to Two-Finger, and Two-Finger slipped him a stack of double eagles.

Mose looked up to see if the stick had the money, then he looked at the cowboy, and spun the wheel. He threw up his arm and covered his eyes as the pointer stopped on a red mark. Then, with one eye on the open gold he stepped to the end of the frame and reached his hand through a slit in the canvas for the stack of gold from the stick, who was well concealed in the darkness. Mose stepped back to the wheel.

"Now, then," he began, and he wasn't working with so much pressure. The stick knew why. Mose had them. He could coast. Mose smoothed his beard carefully. "You've got two hundred and twenty-six dollars there, mister." He strung fifteen double eagles across the board. They made a nice layout. There was a crowd now around the frame. Mose might have to move pretty fast at the kill. "It's all yours. Now, I'll tell you what I'll do. Two-twenty-six will get you five hundred more, if it stops on a red mark again." He was singing now, loud and confident. That meant he really was taking the chump to the laundry.

The cowboy swallowed and nodded. Mose spun the wheel. He put on a very good imitation of a scream when it stopped again on red. He threw down fifteen more double eagles, and by now the board was well loaded. He scattered them so they couldn't be counted too fast later. "Seven hundred and seventy-six dollars," he moaned. "I'm seventy-five short, mister. I'll send out for the big boss." He motioned imperiously to Two-Finger. "A stack!" he shouted.

Two-Finger dropped five double eagles into a small boy's hand and watched him go across the open space. The boy handed the coins to Mose with his eyes almost as big as the gold pieces. "Thank you, sonny. Thank you very much. How does it feel to have a whole bank in your hands? Now, then, people . . . wait a minute." He had seen a doubt in the big cowboy's eyes, and he didn't dare hesitate. "Where's the gentleman who put up your first dollar for you? You yourself wouldn't put up but five dollars, you know." He was well aware that the big cowboy squirmed at that statement before his neighbors. "You," Mose said to the stick, who appeared again in the light. "You've got nineteen dollars change coming. How about it? You want to let it ride at two for one on the next bet?"

The stick nodded, and Mose went on: "You're the one that started this phenomenal streak of luck in the first place, and you haven't even got your original dollar back. You're entitled to win something. Isn't he?" he asked the big cowboy.

The cowboy nodded, his eyes on the pile of gold.

"Now, madam," Mose said to the girl as he dropped five gold pieces on the table, "you don't want your man to be a cheapskate, do you? No, I thought not. You look like a mighty sensible girl. You've got a good man, and you're proud of him, aren't you? Sure. He's making money hand over fist here. It's better than the United States mint. What do you say?" He started to spin. "Seven-seventy-six will get you fifteen hundred, mister. Do we spin?"

Then he stopped and looked up. He took off his tall hat and scratched his bald head and did his best to look confused. "Something's wrong here, mister. You've got nearly eight hundred dollars, plus nineteen you're letting ride to pay the kind gentleman back for starting you on this phenomenal streak of luck. But you haven't put up a nickel. Now you stand to win fifteen hundred dollars . . . and, when this hand is played, gentlemen, I'm through. Now, look, mister, you've been playing with my money against me. Seven hundred and seventy-one dollars. You stand to make twenty-three hundred dollars." He looked up sharply. "If you lose, can you pay off?"

"What do you mean?" asked the cowboy.

"When you play a hand of poker without any money on the table, and you win, you have to show your own money before you collect, don't you?"

The big cowboy nodded.

"You wouldn't deny me that satisfaction, would you? The honor of a gentleman?" he capped it. "Can you pay off, if you lose?"

Mose's eyes were burning. This would be the biggest kill in months.

The big cowboy swallowed. He moved closer to the table, and his fingers twitched toward the kick in his right back pocket. "I didn't figure. . . ."

"How much can you cover, mister?"

"Well, I . . ."

"Can you cover six hundred?" This was the sell.

"Well, not . . ."

"Can you cover three hundred?"

The roll of currency came out.

"Let's see your money. I trust you, mister, but count it out. Let's be open and aboveboard with each other."

The big cowboy counted out three hundred and sixty-five dollars. No sound came from the close-packed crowd. Every person there was holding his breath.

"O K," said Mose. "Put that three hundred and sixty-five over here in this little love nest with this seven hundred and seventy-six. Now that makes eleven hundred and forty-one. Eleven hundred and forty-one dollars, mister, will get you twenty-five hundred on the red. Isn't that fair enough? You've only got a third of it, and this gentleman here has nineteen, and he wants his money back, and you stand to win twenty-five hundred. You can buy a whole cattle ranch with twenty-five hundred. Now, I'll tell you what I'll do." With a practiced flourish he dropped red cards until seven eighths of the spaces were solid red. "Now there are more red spaces than there are white. How can you lose? You can't ask for odds any better than that, can you? You would not be baby enough for that. Now, mister, I spin the little wheel."

He spun it, and he backed away so the one-eighth without red markers would show up. He lifted his beaver and wiped the sweat from his bald head. The arrow slowed. He watched it. He couldn't afford to make a mistake now that the cowboy had his own money on the board. The little pointer hesitated on a red spot in the one-eighth. Fifty people sucked in their breaths. The big cowboy licked his lips. The girl clung to his arm. Mose lifted his toe. The pointer eased over into the white, and stopped.

Mose was already sweeping the money into his hat. "That's the way it goes, gentlemen. Better luck next time."

The big cowboy was staring at the wheel, stunned. The girl was incredulous. Then she saw that Mose was taking the money, and tears sprang into her eyes. She tried to speak, but choked. She drew a deep breath and turned to the cowboy and said, with her fingers fumbling for his hands: "It's all right, Jim. We'll get along."

She was a swell sport, the stick thought. She was good and sweet and kind. She was a lady, and suddenly the stick knew he couldn't let her take the rap any more than he had let the bearded lady take the rap for the phony money. The stick felt all soft inside for a minute. Then he took a deep breath and stepped up to the counter. "Mister," he said to Mose, "if you had lost . . . could *you* pay off?"

Mose stopped, paralyzed. Finally he turned his bald head and looked at the stick.

"The way I figure it," said the stick, astonished to find that he could still speak with Mose glaring incredulous hatred at him, "you would have owed this gentleman here thirty-six hundred and forty-one dollars, and you would have owed me fifty-seven dollars. That makes almost thirty-seven hundred dollars, mister. Could you pay off, if you had lost?"

Mose took a deep breath. His chest swelled, and murder was in his small eyes, but the stick didn't back away. He knew he'd have to run in a minute, but right now—well, he looked at the girl and saw the sudden shining faith in her blue eyes, and for a moment he wasn't afraid of anybody. "How about it?" he said to Mose. "According to my figures, you've only got seven hundred and eighty-two dollars of your own money up. You're a little short, mister."

This was the first time this game had ever been played from this side of the board. It was bitter, but it was justice.

Mose licked his dry lips and looked desperately toward Two-Finger. Two-Finger shook his head. Mose looked toward Broadway Jones. He, too, shook his head. The stick was exultant. He knew there wasn't that much free money in the whole carnival except for The Man, and The Man wouldn't trust Mose with that kind of money even for a moment. Mose was cornered. His mouth dropped open, and he started for the side of the frame. But the counter crashed behind him from the butt of a big six-shooter in the cowboy's hand.

Mose stopped as if he were frozen, his shoulders hunched together under his black coat, waiting for the bullet. But the big cowboy said in a great, resonant voice: "Where is your money, mister? Can you pay off?"

Mose looked around slowly. He saw the revolver aimed at his chest. His face went white, but he didn't give up. It puzzled the stick to see the cunning that came in Mose's eyes.

Mose set the hat full of money on the counter and spoke doggedly, watching the gun with the sharpness of a desperate rake. "Yes, I can pay off," he said finally. His voice was a croak.

The stick straightened and frowned. What was going on? Mose left the hat full of money on the counter. With the gun on his back, he reached up and took one of the plaster dolls from his flash. He struck it on the edge of the counter and broke off the head. He reached inside and brought out a thick package of flat, new twenty-dollar yellowbacks.

The stick's eyes bulged out. Mose was triumphant as he looked at the cowboy. Then his glance swept around to the stick, and the stick shrank. He started moving back from the cold fury in Mose's eyes.

Somebody was pushing into the crowd. A girl. The stick stared. The spider girl. She walked up to Mose with a small, nickel-plated pistol in her hand and said: "Let me see those bills."

Mose started to run. She fired, and his left arm twitched. He turned back, and he looked like a ghost.

The spider girl snatched the package of yellowbacks. She said to the cowboy: "Watch him." She looked at the top bill, and then thumbed through the package. She looked back up. Her voice was level. "I arrest you," she said, "in the name of the United States government. I'm a Secret Service operator, and these are counterfeit bills."

There was a dead hush. The stick was astounded. He remembered the spider girl had joined the carnival a few days after the federal man had taken his own money. He said timidly: "Miss, I don't understand this."

She had just slipped a pair of handcuffs over Mose's wrists. She snapped them shut and said to Mose: "March out . . . this way." When Mose was in front of the counter, his bald head shining, she smiled at the stick. It was a warm smile, and the stick felt good. "There's been a trail of bad bills following this carnival all summer, but we couldn't put our finger on the source. Then, when we heard about the phony federal man, they sent me. With your help," she said to the stick, "we've caught the passer. He bought a stack of bad money in the East and came out here to pass it off."

"Did you say *phony* federal man?" the stick asked.

"Yes. That wasn't an honest-to-goodness agent at all. That was just somebody Mose sent to get your money away from you so he could go into business." She said with a sudden smile: "How much of your own money did you lose?"

"About twelve hundred."

She reached into Mose's hat. She counted out three hundred and sixty-five and gave it to the cowboy. "Don't bet on the other man's game," she advised. "That wheel is as phony as these bills."

She gave the rest to the stick. "A little quick justice," she said.

"Part of this is Two-Finger's," said the stick.

Two-Finger's booming voice spoke up. "I'll loan it to you, if you want to go back in business."

The stick grinned happily. "I do," he said. Then a thought struck him. "Where's the fellow that said he was a federal man?"

The spider girl looked at him. "Say, by the way, where *did* you get those bad bills . . . or were there any?"

"I guess there were, but I . . ." He hesitated. He wanted to help the spider girl, but how could he tell on a lady? After all, the lady had trusted him. He raised his head, and his eyes involuntarily came to rest on the picture of the bearded lady across the midway.

The spider girl saw it and moved. With the big cowboy holding a gun on Mose, she ran across the midway. The stick followed her as fast as he could. He was uncomfortable. He had not meant to tell.

The spider girl ran past the ticket man. She swept into the big tent, past the sword swallower, the human skeleton, and the fire-eater, past the cage that held the geek—the wild man from Borneo. To the little platform where the bearded lady sat.

There was no bearded lady there now. Her chair was empty. And on the floor of the platform was a false beard of black hair, crumpled where she had stepped on it.

The stick looked at the beard and said sadly: "I always wondered if she were real."

# The Coming Home

Mark Draper rode slowly, his long legs slack, his feet hanging loosely in the stirrups, his thoughts unsettled. Here he was, nearly home, but things weren't adding up right; the last four miles were stringing out longer than the first nineteen hundred. It had seemed simple enough, when he had left San Antonio. He would walk the gelding into the yard, tie up to the corral fence, walk around the barn, and say quietly: "Well, Dad, I'm back. I think I've learned a few things." And then they would shake hands firmly, and everything would be all right between them.

But he had hardly pulled out of the rodeo grounds in San Antonio when that assurance had deserted him, and he had begun to wonder just what he *had* learned. He had thought maybe his mind would clear when he got lined out on the way home, but it didn't. The unsureness grew on him all the way, and finally at Selden, four miles from the end of the trip, it had come all over him like a saddle blanket dropped over a cricket.

He had ridden through the small town, noting that the hitch rack had been removed from alongside the post office. No one recognized him, he guessed—or maybe they had but had not wanted to speak. He was not relieved when he rode up the hill past the water tower and then turned left down a graded dirt road. He wished he had not come back at all, for suddenly all the things he had put behind him in the last four years had risen up without warning to plague him: Archie Warton and his sneakiness, the moving of the turkey houses, his father's cold hardness when he had told him to get out—and Caroline Bird's clinging good-bye kiss.

Then the bay began to pick up its ears, but Mark sat back in the saddle and held the reins against it. All those thoughts and many more—all of them unspoken—seemed to be rolling up like sod before a breaking plow—but they didn't curve over to one side in a crisp black ribbon, but rather seemed to pile up before him until he had to push a way through with both hands, like a man swimming through thick mud.

The sun was low in the west, almost resting on the white caps of the mountains, and for a little while, as the gelding walked along the dirt road, the birdcalls and the crickets' chirping and the deer flies' buzzing seemed to hush, waiting for the change from day to night. Then he heard hogs grunting in the meadow to the left. Hogs never paid attention to anything else if there was something to eat, he noted.

He looked left. Old Pete Warton's place was shin-deep in alfalfa, dusty green and loaded with purple blossoms, and rooting along in it was a drove of white-belted Hampshires, half hidden and well satisfied.

It had been just the right kind of day—cool in the shade of the waxy-leaved elm trees but warm in the sun. Up the slope on the right, each apple tree in the Bird orchard seemed to grow out of a pool of pink and white, and, as he looked, the last warm breeze of the day rustled through the orchard and left a slow shower of fluttering petals. Mark took a deep breath, soothing his troubled thoughts with the honest smell of freshly turned black earth, of lilacs in bloom, of the light sweat on the gelding's withers. It was a good country, and his being there should have been good—but now he didn't know.

He reached the bridge over the irrigation ditch. A pair of orioles chased each other across the road in swooping golden-orange arcs, and the gelding's hoofs clumped hollowly on the wood of the bridge. The ditch was running full; there must have been plenty of snow in the mountains. The gelding reached the highest part of the rounded floor of the bridge, and Mark saw Caroline Bird.

She had come up the inside of the fence, under cover of the trees and partly hidden by the castor beans that Elmer Bird always planted along the fence. She sat her big black stallion and gazed up at Mark with softly questioning brown eyes.

He straightened and sat tall in the saddle as the gelding cantered down off the bridge and swished through deep grass up to the fence. He pushed his big hat to the back of his head, suddenly aware that his sun-bleached brown hair was shaggy and needed cutting. He sat there, taking her in. The four years seemed like four thousand, and for a moment speaking was impossible.

She broke the silence with an abrupt question: "What's wrong, Mark?"

He felt the uneasiness in her voice and saw a tiny line appear between her eyes. He must have stared at her too hungrily. He forced his eyes to break from hers. He looked her over quickly, taking in her well-worn jeans, her plaid wool shirt, the calfskin vest he had tanned and made for her on her nineteenth birthday, the tall, light-brown Stetson that miraculously stayed on top of a mass of glossy black curls. He looked back at her questioning dark eyes, and then he realized with abruptness and new force that he had left home under harsh circumstances, that in his youthful indignation he had not been careful about writing letters, and so now they didn't know what might have happened to him inside—whether he had adjusted himself or whether he had gone sour.

He smiled finally. "The black," he said, "is still a lot of horse." He was rewarded by seeing the line of anxiety fade from between her eyes. A rush of words came to his lips. "It's like a hungry man looking at a plateful of fried chicken . . . seeing you like this. You went all over me and took my breath away . . . even more than you used to."

"Didn't you expect to see me, Mark?" she asked quietly.

"Sure, but . . ." He hesitated. He couldn't tell her that he had doubted. "I guess I wasn't ready for it."

Her voice lifted. "Maybe," she said in her old teasing way, "I'd better take a turn around the orchard while you get your breath back."

"No," he said quickly. "Ride along the fence with me to the corner."

She pivoted the black on his front legs, his tail swishing at a gray-bodied horsefly. They started off at a walk. He watched her from a corner of his eye. He could almost reach across the castor beans and touch her—but there were all those things piled up between them.

"Have things changed very much, Mark?"

She glanced back at him (the black was always a fast walker), and now Mark studied the back of her neck, olive-tan under her black hair. Yes, change had something to do with their standoffishness now. Change—or the possibility of change. Not knowing each other. Four years was a long time. A great many things could have happened. It was that unspoken possibility that lay between them now. Coming back was not like leaving.

"Or does it all look the same?" she asked.

He let the musical huskiness of her voice sink into his bones. On the rodeo circuit he had heard a lot of husky female voices, but none like Caroline's. There had been whiskey voices or cigarette voices or voices from throats used too much for yelling. They had been harsh or coarse—but Caroline's voice was like the soft rustle of the south wind through a tree laden with fruit.

"Yes, it's been forever," he said. "But you haven't changed except . . . to grow prettier." He hesitated over that because he realized, as he said it, that the years had made her into a woman. She was still slim, but she was fuller in the bosom and in the hips. He had learned to notice those things in the four years.

She turned in the saddle to look at him. "You've grown taller, I think, Mark. You're browner than when you left, too."

"That's from riding cattle cars."

"And somehow," she said, "you seem much older."

"I *am* older," he said, his eyes fixed on her.

Unexpectedly she blushed and turned back. The stallion shook its head at a fly, and she said gently: "Where have you come from, Mark?"

"San Antone," he said.

She glanced at him, puzzled. "The last go-'round in San Antone was two months ago."

It made him warm inside to know she had watched the papers. "I didn't hurry," he said. "I stopped off now and then."

"Sometimes I saw your name in the winners," she said, "the last two years."

"I had fair luck. Won pretty good money in the steer wrestling one year, and took enough prizes to keep going . . . better than most of those who break into it cold."

"You always were handy with a rope." She added thoughtfully: "You were a fair rider, too."

"The boys who draw their numbers night after night are all good," he said. "You have to be lucky . . . and I was lucky. The only reason I didn't come all the way home on a train was that I wanted to think."

"Didn't you have plenty of time to think between rodeos?"

"There's never time for thinking around a rodeo. You're always figuring up your points, practicing for the next one, wondering when it'll be your turn in the hospital . . . when you start thinking about something else, you don't last."

There was relief in her voice. "You didn't get hurt, then?"

He shrugged. "Only once. I drew a hatbox bucker in the finals at Cheyenne and got four cracked ribs." He chuckled. "That bull made me three hundred dollars, so I forgave him."

He heard her catch her breath. "You said you'd never ride the Brahmas."

He laughed easily. "There are times you can't be fussy."

They rode in sudden silence. They had been sparring with words, not talking about the things that counted between them. He tried to speak casually: "Who's working for Dad . . . anybody I know?"

"Archie Warton," she said without looking around.

He stiffened in the saddle. The bay's hoofs sawed through the tall grass along the fence.

"Help has been scarce, you know," said Caroline.

Mark wasn't listening. The bay reached down for a mouthful of grass, but Mark jerked its head up. Archie Warton, slick-haired, black eyes too shiny, too wise—especially around girls. It was Archie who had shot the third-grade teacher in the seat with tinfoil—but, when they were searched, the rubber band was found in Mark's hip pocket, and Mark had taken the licking for it. It was Archie who had suggested, the summer of their first year in high school, that they steal peaches from Mrs. Gateley's orchard, but it was Mark who had gotten a load of rock salt in the pants and had nearly gone crazy from the burning.

There were other counts against Archie—like the time Archie and Mark had started smoking. Mark's father had always said: "When you think you've got to smoke, do it in the house or in the open. Don't sneak off behind the barn." But Archie had bought a package of cigarettes and persuaded Mark to try them behind a haystack. The haystack had caught on fire, and Mark's father had stormed about it. "If you'd do what I tell you," he had said, "you'd stay out of trouble."

But Mark had said sullenly: "I'm old enough to do some thinking of my own."

His father had taken off his hat—he always took off his hat when he felt strongly about something—and a wisp of white hair stood up like a cowlick. "You're old enough," his father had said bluntly. "But what you think doesn't make sense."

Mark had bristled. "Who's got the right to say what makes sense?"

His father had glared at him, snorted, and turned away.

The next day had been Saturday, and his father was going into town for some turkey poults. "That young Higgins boy is coming over to help you set up the turkey houses. He'll show you where to put them. I'm going by the bank, and I won't pick up the turkeys until this afternoon, so you'll have plenty of time."

Young Higgins had come across the field right after Mark's father left, and Mark had met him at the barn. "Here are the frames," Mark had said. "All we have to do is haul them to the high ground up there and put them together."

Higgins was a sandy-haired Irishman. "Your father said to put them on the slope down near the creek," he had told Mark.

Mark had glared at him. "Whose farm do you think this is?"

Higgins had said no more, but when Mark's father had reached home near sundown with sixteen hundred turkey poults on the truck, he had cursed when he had seen the turkey houses. "I told young Higgins to put them on the slope."

Mark had said righteously: "You didn't tell me."

His father's callused, work-cracked hands had clenched into fists. "No," he had said slowly, "I didn't tell you. I know you wouldn't do what I wanted anyway."

"I didn't figure they should be so low," Mark had argued. "It might flood."

"You been wantin' to think," his father had said pointedly. "This was a good time to start. You've lived here all your life. You know there's not enough snow in the hills to flood the slope this year." He had taken off his hat. "If you had any sense, you'd have remembered we ran the turkeys on the high ground last fall."

But Mark had refused to be cowed. "The turkeys are half mine," he had said. "I've got as much interest as you have."

His father had said finally: "It's too late to change them now. We'll start them out on the high ground and hope for the best."

The best hadn't been very good. The young

poults had broken out with sickness picked up from the fouled ground, and two-fifths of them died. Mark's father had said disgustedly: "I hope you've learned your lesson."

But then there was the second summer after high school, when Archie went into town to find a girl to go with, and Mark was beginning to think of marrying Caroline. That second summer Mark's father bought a registered Holstein bull, and he told Mark: "Whatever you do, don't monkey with that bull. He seems gentle enough . . . but I've got four thousand dollars tied up in that animal, and I can't afford to lose it."

It was Archie then who dreamed up the idea of a home-talent rodeo in the meadow, and Archie who suggested the bull would make a good substitute for a Brahma. But Mark would never forget the whiteness around his father's mouth as he ran clumsily, hat in hand, into the meadow that Sunday afternoon. Mark slid off the bull's back and faced him, a little weak in the knees even though he was tall and tough-muscled and scared of nobody.

His father grabbed the bull's halter. "You must be a fool as well as a nincompoop," he shouted at Mark, "to ride a registered bull."

Mark caught his breath. Then he said easily: "I can take care of myself. He won't hurt me."

His father exploded. "Who's worrying about you? If you get a broken leg, you can go to the hospital. If the bull gets a broken leg, I might have to shoot him."

A wisp of white hair stood up from the top of his father's head; his blue eyes were glaring. He snorted at Mark.

Mark tried to be indignant. "So you figure the bull's leg is worth more than mine."

Slowly the glare left his father's eyes. A different look came in them. It was quieter but somehow harder than anger, and Mark was shaken.

"Come on home," his father said coldly, slamming his hat on his head.

His father led the bull, and Mark followed, watching his father's clumsy gait and growing more and more rebellious, for after all he was nineteen and through school and thinking of getting married. They reached the barn. His father stopped outside the gate, still holding the bull's halter. He looked long and carefully at Mark, seeming to search his face, and said heavily: "You're almost twenty, Mark. I reckon the old place is too familiar to you . . . and they say familiarity breeds contempt."

Mark's answer was sullen. It was burning him up because, as usual, Archie had started it, but Archie wasn't getting blamed—but he wouldn't say that. "I had to follow you home like a kid." His father stared at him but did not immediately reply, and Mark felt encouraged to go on. "I do a man's work. I want to be treated like a man."

"You work, all right, but you've never acted like a grownup. No man in his right mind would use a high-priced breeding bull for a rodeo critter." He drew a deep breath. "You don't like my telling you things. You want to make up your own rules as you go along."

"As you said," Mark pointed out, "I'm nearly twenty. I don't see why I have to be at somebody's apron strings all my life." He hoped his voice expressed the resentment he felt.

"The trouble with you is, you've grown up in this valley, around this town, on this farm . . . and you've come to take everything for granted. You've never learned that everybody has to take orders from somebody else."

Mark swelled up, but his father didn't notice.

His father's blue eyes seemed to look through him without seeing him. "I figure it's time for you to get out by yourself, where people won't *let* you take advantage of them. It's the only way some boys ever get the rough edges knocked off."

Mark stared. He swallowed and asked: "What do you mean?"

His father's eyes seemed far away and swimming in Mark's vision. His hat was in his gnarled hands again. "A boy at home lives in a little world all his own. He doesn't know he's got to adjust to the world, and not the world to him. You don't want me to tell you anything . . . even around the farm." His mouth tightened, and he glanced down. "You're too soft-handed for a farmer. I reckon it's time for you to move out, Mark."

It hit Mark like a sackful of sand on the top of his head. For a moment he was emotionally numb from the blow, then it spread through his body, and it was as if the weight was still on his head, growing heavier, pressing him down. He wished he could sit, but there was nothing to sit on.

His father went ahead a few steps and opened the gate to the pasture. He turned the bull inside, unsnapped the halter rope, and closed the gate. He stood there for a moment, watching the bull walk off toward the creek. He turned and came back in his usual clumsy gait. Mark started to say something resentful, but his rebellion deserted him. He kept still.

"Remember this," his father said. "It's not the going away that'll do you good, but the things that happen inside of you, the things you learn . . . and how you take it when you learn them."

Mark tried to joke. He knew before he said it that it wasn't going to be funny, but he didn't know what else to do. He'd never considered being away from home, and somehow the thought seemed to jerk everything out from under him. "You want me to send you a telegram when I find out all these things?" he asked.

"You won't find them out until you come back. It isn't the going away," he said emphatically, "but the coming back."

Mark felt sick. He wished he had left on his own initiative, but now it was too late. "What can I work at?" he asked, more to have an answer than anything else. He was wondering what Caroline would say.

"You're a good rider and roper," his father said, "and you've got a good horse. Why don't you tackle rodeo?"

It wasn't a very subtle idea, Mark thought, but he saw his father was in earnest. Mark took a deep breath. "All right," he said abruptly. "I'll hit for Calgary in the morning. The Stampede starts Monday."

His father nodded, releasing a long breath. "You've got two months' wages coming. It'll give you a start."

Mark gave him a short, hard glance. He had a

glimpse of his father, putting on his hat slowly, as he turned away. He thought his father looked a little white under his weatherbeaten skin, but he didn't give it any attention. He was through. He had been kicked out. He didn't belong to this place anymore.

About sundown, after he packed an old suitcase, he got on the gelding and went up to see Caroline. She rode down through the apple orchard to meet him. She was wearing the calfskin vest, and her dark eyes were clouded. "I hear there was an awful row, Mark."

"You hear fast," he said dryly.

Her long, smoothly sun-browned fingers combed the stallion's thick black mane. "What did he say, Mark?"

Mark's words exploded in sudden bitterness. "He kicked me out!"

She did not seem as astonished as he had expected. "What else happened?" she asked.

"Isn't that enough?"

Then they were standing between their horses, and he was holding her to him desperately. "I'm not going to ask you to wait," he whispered into her fragrant hair, "but if you're here when I come back . . ."

She leaned against his arms and studied his face in the deepening shadows. Abruptly her eyes were red with tears. She buried her head on his shoulder and cried softly. He caressed the back of her head with his hand.

"I like your hands, Mark," she said.

He looked at his smooth hands at her back. His

father had said he was too soft-handed to be a farmer, but Caroline said she liked them. He guessed his father had been pretty mad.

She lifted her face. "Take care of yourself, Mark."

She kissed him good bye. Her lips were salty. He felt the warmth and firmness of them, and he didn't want to leave. But his father had ordered him out; he had no choice. Then he remembered his father's solicitude for the bull, and it stiffened him.

The entry fees at Calgary took a large part of his money, but he did not win any of it back. He went to the smaller towns, but he was almost broke before he won some prize money. He dropped to Brahma riding because the entry fee was usually under five dollars, and there he found the competition not quite as tough. At a little town down in Idaho, where they didn't even have a grandstand, he won twenty-five dollars and got a job tending a carful of rodeo stock for his and the gelding's transportation to the next date.

He wrote his father once, but he didn't get an immediate answer. Maybe mail had trouble finding him on the broken-bones circuit, or maybe his father was too busy worrying about his precious bull. Mark wrote Caroline once, too, but her answer, by airmail, mentioned a square dance and how "Archie Warton was cutting up like a big clown." He didn't write Caroline after that. He'd had enough of Archie Warton to last him a lifetime. He wondered if Archie and Caroline were going together.

He followed the circuit east through Wyoming. He caught the tail end of Frontier Days at Cheyenne, but he couldn't enter anyway; the fees were too high. He rode the bay ninety-three miles up to Torrington, sleeping in his saddle blanket on the prairie to save money.

He lay there one night, with the everlasting wind driving fine sand through the blanket and into his clothes, leaving a fine powder of dust over his entire body, and he thought of Archie Warton, sleeping in a clean bed at home. Archie had always been a promoter, but he was sharp enough to get out from under while somebody else took the blame. Generally that somebody else had been Mark Draper.

Mark's resentment began to wane. He forgot it long enough to hit his lick at the Torrington rodeo. It wasn't a big show, but the stock was salty, and some of the competition, coming up from the Cheyenne contests, was high-caliber. Nevertheless Mark made a hundred and forty dollars.

It was there he first ran into Slim Junipher. Slim was six feet one and slender as a blade of grass. He whipped like a steel spring when he rode a bucking horse, but he knew that balance was the basis of riding, and he had it. He spoke to Mark back of the calf pen on the final day. "You'll make a fair hand, young fellow."

Mark was cleaning out the frog on the gelding's near front foot. "Thanks," he said.

"What are you in this business for, anyway?"

Mark looked up. He'd been thinking about that. "I want to win enough to buy my own farm," he said, squinting into the sun. "If there's any orders given, I want to give them."

Slim nodded. "Like me. I want a ranch down in Colorado." He sat down on his heels and began delicately to split a stem of straw with his jackknife. "Trouble is, the only way you can win enough money for that is to get into the big shows... Cheyenne, Madison Square Garden, Denver, Fort Worth, San Antone, San Francisco. That's where the money is. The winners in the steer roping at Cheyenne this year divvied up nearly five thousand dollars."

"That's my kind of money," said Mark.

"Trouble is, you can't enter those shows without money. Costs a hundred dollars to get in that steer roping. You can easy spend two or three hundred dollars on entry fees in a big show."

Remembering Calgary, Mark said slowly: "Yes."

"The thing to do," said Slim, "is work into it gradually. Play the little ones, save your money, get experience. Work on the bulls and the barebacks. The entry fees are low because a man can easy get hurt, but the prizes aren't bad, and, if you keep your nose clean, you can get some money ahead and give one of the big ones a whirl once in a while just to get the feel of it. You'll lose your entry fees, and then you can go back to the tank towns and start building up again." He stood up tall. "You'll make a hand," he repeated, "but don't try to go too fast."

"Thanks," said Mark.

He didn't even sit in the stud game that night after the show was over. The next day he started the swing east along the Platte, nursing his money through Nebraska, then south through Kansas and Oklahoma. He'd show them all; he'd buy a farm of his own, and he'd run it his way.

It was tough going down on the hot, dusty prairies of the Great Plains, and he began to hate Archie again, who in a sense was responsible for it. His hate was casual at first, and then, as the fall came early and the winds were cold out of the northwest, his hate grew. He went west for the fall shows, and, when he had to make a long ride in a boxcar with only the blanket to keep him warm, his hate became a slow, smoldering fire. At Christmas he was stranded in Tucson, and he found it no place for a stray cowhand without a job. His hate became a gnawing thing that winter.

He started out again in February. For a long time he hated Archie, and for a long time he barely made enough to eat and to feed the gelding. Most of the time he sat on the top of the fence near the bucking chutes or stood just inside, pretending to study the animals, but thinking more about Archie Warton and Caroline and his dad.

At Tulsa, Slim Juniper, a money winner that year, rode out on a big purple bareback broncho called Loco Weed; Slim had his lick that summer and was riding everything but the vile-tempered Brahmas. Loco Weed was big and squarehipped like a plow horse. He tucked his head between his feet and humped his back; he went up high and came down stiff-legged and hard, and Slim slid off the rump. Loco Weed let go with both hind feet as Slim rolled down. He caught Slim in the back and lifted him up, then dropped him facedown in the sour-smelling turf. Slim lay, and the boys along the fence were on their feet. The pickup man was cutting in, and the stretcher-men were running out

from under the announcer's stand, when Loco
Weed unexpectedly wheeled and started for Slim.

Mark yelled. He sprinted toward Slim, waving
his hat and yelling at the horse. Loco Weed veered.
Then the pickup man rode alongside and crowded
him toward the receiving pen.

That evening Mark was forking hay into the
Mexican steers' lot when Slim limped over from a
taxi. Slim took his hand and held it a long time.
"That damn' Loco Weed!" he said.

Mark looked away. "Don't mention it," he said.

Slim hung over the fence and watched Mark fork
the hay. "That Loco Weed's a horse, all right. He'll
give you a good ride . . . but I saw him try that stunt
at Cheyenne a couple of years ago. They'll outlaw
him if he keeps it up." Slim was chewing a stem of
alfalfa. "I don't mind a horse taking a good healthy
kick. That's what makes bareback riding interest-
ing. But when they turn around and come back after
you . . ."

Mark clipped the wires on a bale of hay and
watched it spring out endwise when the pressure
was released. "You're lucky he didn't get you in
the spine."

"Mighty lucky," Slim said reflectively. He watched
a muley steer try to climb the fence. "Funny about a
horse like that. Just like some people. Here he is a
rodeo bronc', and that's a soft spot for a horse if there
ever was one . . . but what does he do? He resents it.
And what'll it get him? A job hauling a beer wagon if
he's lucky. Like a lot of people. They can be sittin'
pretty, but they take a notion they don't like it, and
they try to make things over instead of fittin' in.

Them kind generally find they've got their work cut out."

Mark tossed a big forkful of hay onto the back of a dun steer.

Slim looked at him sidewise. "I been watchin' you, kid. You got the reputation of bein' a lone wolf. But you're O K or you wouldn't have run out to help me." He paused. "Something's wrong," he said earnestly. "I been watchin' you since we left Alamosa. Is it a girl?"

"No."

"Then it's a man," Slim said shrewdly. "Somebody done you dirt."

"Yes."

Slim took a deep breath. "You'll have to get over it. That's what's the matter with old Loco Weed. He's broodin' over something. Maybe a drunk cowboy beat him over the head with a bridle once."

Mark looked up quickly. "Would you blame him?"

"That ain't the point. You just can't afford to go around rememberin' things like that. Life's too short . . . and around a rodeo it'll get shorter than ever if you spend your energy hating somebody."

Mark said: "I'm all right."

"Your mind ain't on your business," Slim insisted. "Something's eatin' on you. You better go back and get it straightened up before you go too far."

Mark looked away over the feedlots. A dozen cowpunchers were forking hay out of broken bales and tossing it over fences. His eyes turned northwest. Home was a long way off.

"Hope you're O K tomorrow, Slim," he said at last.

Mark finished the season, broke, in Utah, and got a job on a Wyoming ranch to save money for the opening of the next season. He went out with a sheep wagon for three months and tried to forget Archie. It was hard, but he made progress, and that year he did better all along the line. At the end of the year, however, he was no nearer a farm than ever. He was still constantly scratching for entrance fees for the big shows. He splurged in October to wind up the season at the Cow Palace in San Francisco. He didn't win anything there, and, when it was over, he was broke again, but he had come a long way, and in the light of his progress he thought it fair to assume that his hatred for Archie was gone. He felt differently toward his father, too, and he wondered if Caroline was married yet.

The next year Loco Weed was dropped from the rodeo string; an Iowa farmer was going to try to make a plow horse out of him. That year Mark went into the arena to win contests. He began to take prizes at the big shows, and in between he traveled hard and took all the small money he could get. He wound up at the Boston Gardens in November.

Boston was cold and bleak that year. He went to Mexico to work the two winter months. They still handled their cattle rough down in Sinaloa, and he got in some good practice.

He started his fourth season in Fort Worth, entering everything, going all out to win, and netting nearly twelve hundred dollars. For once, that was clear. It was also that year that handlers were high-priced and scarce, and the rodeo contestants, to assure their own safety without cutting down their prize money, took turns at the chutes and at the pens and as pickup men in the arena. It didn't bother Mark, for they usually did that at the smaller shows anyway.

At San Antonio, Mark took the first day-money in steer wrestling (he had learned the tricks of the Mexican steers by that time), one day-money in broncho riding, a third place in bull riding, and two firsts in calf roping.

When those not disqualified gathered in the horse barn the night before the finals to draw their animals for the last day, Slim Juniper slapped Mark on the back. "You're off to a championship this year," he said. "I feel it coming on." He said in a lower voice: "Whatever it was eating you three years ago in Tulsa, it looks like you got it fixed up."

Mark nodded soberly. "It looks like I've got my lick this year."

A cowboy holding a tall hat upside down called: "Draper, pick your horse."

Mark took a capsule out of the hat. It had a small piece of paper folded inside. He unfolded it.

"Eighteen," he told Slim.

Slim said: "Lemme see." He examined it. He handed it back to Mark, grinning. "You're going to make a lot of money," he said, "or you're gonna get throwed."

"What's the horse?"

"High Noon."

Mark gulped. "I thought they saved High Noon for exhibition rides."

Slim shook his head. "They don't have exhibition rides in the big shows any more. They use the big buckers in the finals. Horse counts forty percent, remember?"

Mark grinned. "I guess I'm lucky."

"It's your year," said Slim. "High Noon is one of the greatest bucking horses since Cal Coolidge and Made in Germany. There isn't a rider here who wouldn't give two hundred dollars to be in your place. He's been rode just three times in four years. You drawed yourself a place in the money."

Mark nodded thoughtfully, trying to adjust himself to the awesome reputation of High Noon.

"You stand to make a pile in calf roping, too, if you don' run into bad luck."

"My average time is sixteen two seconds."

"Well, get a good night's sleep," Slim counseled. "That horse will take all you've got, but remember . . . there never was a horse who couldn't be rode. And if you ride him, you'll ride into the big money. High Noon is a hard, fast bucker. Nothing fancy, no hard feelings. Does his job and then forgets it. Don't forget, there's three hundred dollars trophy to the champion bronc' rider and five hundred for grand champion cowboy. That High Noon can ride you into a farm in ten seconds."

The next day the sun was hot enough to fry steak, and there was no wind. A horse's hoofs kicked up little mushrooms of dust in the arena, and they hung where they rose until they sifted back down. Mark left the gelding in the shade as long as he could. He had been disqualified in bareback riding, but they called him to act as pickup man. Then the calf roping got under way.

When his calf was run into the chute, Mark lined up on the other side, his loop ready, his pigging string in his teeth. Good time on this calf was worth almost as much as a ride on High Noon, but he didn't think about it. He watched the tape.

The calf shot from the chute. The gelding stood on its hind legs, eager to go, but Mark held it. The calf crossed the thirty-foot line. The tape snapped, high into the air. Mark held back for an instant to let it clear, then he let the gelding surge after the calf. He made a quick catch and went hand over hand down the rope, the gelding holding it taut. He threw the calf, gathered three legs, and started to wrap the string around them. But the calf made an unexpected effort to get free. He kicked two legs loose. It took a few seconds to get things under control, but Mark made the tie and signaled.

He stood by the calf. The judge rode up and dismounted. He turned the calf over. The calf tried to kick, but the tie held. The judge stood there for a moment. The sun was like a furnace at Mark's back. Then the judge nodded, and Mark was relieved. He leaned over and whipped off the string, loosened his loop, and let the calf up. He figured he had been about ten seconds slow on that one, which would make twenty-six seconds, but his average was still pretty good, and it might even win first money.

The judge was a lean, thin-faced, sour-mouthed man in a black hat. He got back on his horse and wrote something in a notebook. "A little slow," he commented. "And I'm adding ten seconds for breaking the tape."

Mark was coiling his rope. He stiffened and looked up. "You what?" he demanded.

"Ten seconds for breaking the tape."

"What tape?" Mark growled.

The judge didn't even answer. He trotted away, leaving the puffs of dust that hung in the air.

Mark saw blazing red. If the man had stayed, Mark would have climbed him. As it was, Mark stood there for a moment, grinding his teeth. Then he heard the time: "Thirty-six seconds." He swung on the bay and rode savagely for the exit gate.

Slim met him. "Ease it off," he said. "Tough luck."

Mark spit the words through his teeth. "What are you talking about?"

"It was a technical foul," said Slim. "Not your fault. The tape looped up and caught on your stirrup. It's a foul under the rules."

Mark glared across the arena at the judge.

"Listen," said Slim. "Don't let this get you down. You've still got every chance in the world to make a killing. Get hold of yourself. You're through now till the bronc' riding, aren't you?"

Mark said sullenly: "Yes."

"It's my turn to work the gate at the receiving pen, but I've got a bull up there with my name on it. Want to take over for me? Give you a chance to work off steam before you make the big ride."

Mark, watching the judge trot up to where another calf was down, nodded slowly. "O K. I'll handle the gate for you."

Mark rode the gelding around to the receiving pen. He tied the horse there in the shade and climbed the fence. In No. 3 chute they had tied the rope around the first bull and hung a big brass cowbell under the bull's belly. The rider got on and grabbed the surcingle with his right hand, held his left high above his head. "Let 'er out," he said. The gate swung back, leaving the bull's left side to the arena. The bull didn't move. A cowboy jabbed him in the flank with an electric prod. The bull erupted. The cowboy was left on the ground just outside of the chute. The bull curved to the right toward the receiving pen gate.

Mark swung the gate wide, keeping himself behind it. The bull went inside. The man at the bull pen gate was slow getting it open. The bull stood there, head lowered, switching his tail. Mark waited, watching the bull, keeping quiet. He would not try to close the gate until the bull was in the right pen, because the bulls, for all their big bulk, were light on their feet and faster than anything on the grounds. They were spooky, too, and anything at all might send the bull charging back into the arena. That was one thing no rodeo man wanted—a loose bull in the arena.

Mark watched. Then the man who was supposed to be watching the bull pen gate got up suddenly from where he had been kneeling at a game of blackjack on the ground outside the pen. He let the bull through and closed the gate.

"Get on the ball there!" Mark yelled through the rising roar of the crowd for another wishful rider.

The hand grinned and thumbed his nose at Mark as Mark closed his own gate.

Slim came out on a big Brahma that was almost white. He was a good bull, and Slim rode him into the money. In fact, Slim was having such a good time that he rode the bull far past the gun for the pickup man was slow—and didn't slide off until the bull was going through Mark's gate. Mark shook hands with him. "You made a ride," he said warmly.

"Looked good to me," Slim said. "I was the last bull rider." He dusted the seat of his Levi's. "You can head for the chutes. Bronc' riding next. I've got to get a drink of water, but I'll be back in plenty of time to watch the gate." He turned away.

Mark was standing with his back to the gate. He started to walk toward the chutes. Then the field judge came by—the man who had penalized Mark ten seconds on his calf. Mark looked at his sour, turned-wrong-side-out lips, and he still didn't like him.

"Put the bolt in that gate!" the judge snapped. "Want to get somebody killed?"

Mark stiffened instantly. He didn't like the judge's tone. "I'm handling the gate," he snapped.

The judge wheeled his horse and rode off without looking back. Mark glared at him. He felt the hot gorge of anger rise through his head. The gate was shut, wasn't it? Who was a field judge, to be giving him orders?

The loudspeaker bellowed out: "Ladies and gentlemen, the next event will be the finals in bronc' riding. And for the first ride, the boys tell me the drawing has brought up what well may be the feature attraction of the year. Mark Draper, top contender for grand champion honors at this show, a young man who has come all the way in four years, will attempt to ride High Noon, the grandest bucking horse in America today. Ladies and gentlemen, the fireworks!"

Up in chute No. 2, they were putting the saddle

on High Noon. Mark, with his heavy horsehide chaps buckled around his waist, squatted on the top of the heavy-boarded chute, watching every move. High Noon was a beautiful horse—strawberry roan with white points, tall (maybe sixteen-and-a-half hands high), slim, deep-chested, intelligent. There was no wildness in his eyes. He stood quietly while they cinched up the saddle from between the boards of the chute sides. One of the winners in bull riding put the halter on and dropped the single grass rope over the horse's neck. "Your stirrups right?" he called to Mark.

Mark, intent on the saddling, grunted. "They're O K," he said.

Another hand threw the flank strap over the horse's croup and fished for the far end with a hook through the boards. "You ready?" he asked Mark, looking up.

Across the arena, the big crowd hushed, waiting.

"Ready," Mark said. His heart was hammering; his voice sounded like someone else's. But he knew he had it. Outside of a fluke, he'd ride the horse that day.

He straddled the chute. The hand buckled the flank strap with a quick movement. Mark dropped into the saddle. He had the halter rope in his left hand. He swung his hat with his right, his eyes on the horse's ears. "O K," he yelled. "Pour 'im out. Let's see if I can ride 'im."

Those were his words before he launched into the ride that was to make him one of the immortals of cowboy land by riding High Noon under association rules—and which was also to be the last ride ever made on the big red horse.

The gate swung wide. High Noon's side was to the arena. He jumped with his front legs and pivoted on his hindquarters. He stuck his bill into the wind and surged from the chute like a jet engine. He reached for dirt with his forelegs, stretched and shivered, came down hard on his hindquarters, arched his back into the air, with his head tucked between his legs and his ears out of sight. He gave a corkscrew twist that started at his withers and went back through his barrel. He flicked his hindquarters to right and left, and was already reaching out with his forelegs again—and all in about half a second. He was one of the fastest bucking horses in rodeo.

Mark rode easily, keeping his balance, watching High Noon's ears when he could see them, looking for a twitch in the shoulder muscles that would telegraph the horse's next move. While he kept his eyes down, he held his left arm before him, free of leather, and scratched the horse down both sides with his spurs, first on the shoulders, then on the flanks. He kept his hat in his right hand, slapping the big red on the side, yelling at every jump. High Noon had brought the big crowd to its feet, and if ever there was a three-hundred-point performance, Mark figured this was the time for it.

The horse veered to the receiving pen gate. A full-throated yell arose finally from the grandstand. Mark thought he heard the ten-second pistol, but he wasn't sure. He kept spurring, slapping, and riding. He didn't see the pickup man alongside, and he didn't want to take a chance.

They neared the big gate at the end of the arena. The pickup man still wasn't there. Then the roar of the crowd died on a single note, and there was a sound that reached Mark like a giant-size gasp. He had heard it before, and now it chilled him, because many times that had been followed by the preacher's "ashes to ashes." He glanced up a little. A bull was coming into the arena—the white bull Slim had ridden. Its big head was high; it moved alertly. The gate banged back as the big shoulder hit it, and the bull trotted out into the arena.

Mark concentrated on the horse. The pickup man still wasn't there—perhaps having misjudged the horse's direction—and to be thrown now would mean hitting the turf in front of the bull.

The horse saw the bull, too, and turned toward the fence before the grandstand. He was still bucking, but less vigorously. Mark looked for the judge and saw that he had turned and ridden back toward the announcing stand, undoubtedly because the ride was over.

The bull had his head still high, but he was running faster, toward them. A lot of the horse's movement was still vertical. The bull was close. He lowered his head with the deceiving, cow-like eyes. Mark considered dropping off to save the horse. He looked for the pickup man. He found him, coming at a hard gallop, trying to intercept them. Two other men were riding out fast from the direction of the calf pens, but they were a long way off.

Mark knew that if he left the horse, High Noon would straighten out and start running. He began to turn loose. The bull was only ten feet away. Mark went off on the side next to the fence.

He lit rolling, but the bull followed the horse. He saw High Noon straighten out into a gallop just as the bull closed up and ripped a long gash in the horse's belly. The horse squealed—that high, terrified sound like the scream of a woman—and bolted against the fence. Mark was on his feet. He started for the bull first, not knowing what he could do but desperate to save the horse from further injury.

The bull hesitated, started to turn back. Mark skinned up the fence. He stopped astraddle of a two-by-six, breathing hard, conscious of the turf dust in his nostrils. He brushed the loose straw off the seat of his Levi's automatically, and became aware of hand-clapping applause—partly in recognition of his ride and partly in relief that he had not been injured. They didn't know yet that High Noon had been gored. He raised a hand in acknowledgment, but his heart wasn't in it. He watched the bull and the horse.

High Noon had stopped, panting, against the fence. Blood dripped from the cut in his belly.

A pickup man cut in between Mark and the bull. "Watch it, cowhand! You can't do any good in there."

The rodeo clown had rolled his barrel at the bull, and the bull stopped to nose it. A rope settled over his horns. A pickup man spurred alongside and hit the bull across the rump with the doubled end of his lariat. The judge and the rodeo manager closed in on the frightened bucking horse and got the halter rope. The bull started for the pens. They let him go. A veterinary was running across the arena on foot.

Slim Junipher came up to Mark and put a hand on his shoulder. "Take it easy," he said. "You got the look in your eyes of a locoed steer."

# GET
# 4 FREE BOOKS!

You can have the best Westerns delivered to your door for less than what you'd pay in a bookstore or online. Sign up for one of our book clubs today, and we'll send you **4 FREE\* BOOKS**, worth $23.96, just for trying it out...with no obligation to buy, ever!

---

Authors include classic writers such as
**LOUIS L'AMOUR, MAX BRAND, ZANE GREY**
and more; PLUS new authors such as
**COTTON SMITH, TIM CHAMPLIN, JOHNNY D. BOGGS**
and others.

---

As a book club member you also receive the following special benefits:

- **30% OFF all orders through our website & telecenter!**
- **Exclusive access to special discounts!**
- **Convenient home delivery and 10 days to return any books you don't want to keep.**

**There is no minimum number of books to buy,**
and you may cancel membership at any time.
**See back to sign up!**

\*Please include $2.00 for shipping and handling.

# YES! ☐

Sign me up for the Leisure Western Book Club
and send my FOUR FREE BOOKS! If I choose to stay
in the club, I will pay only $14.00* each month,
a savings of $9.96!

NAME: _____

ADDRESS: _____

_____

TELEPHONE: _____

E-MAIL: _____

☐ I WANT TO PAY BY CREDIT CARD.

☐ VISA     ☐ MasterCard     ☐ DISCOVER

ACCOUNT #: _____

EXPIRATION DATE: _____

SIGNATURE: _____

Send this card along with $2.00 shipping & handling to:

**Leisure Western Book Club
1 Mechanic Street
Norwalk, CT 06850-3431**

Or fax (must include credit card information!) to: 610.995.9274.
You can also sign up online at www.dorchesterpub.com.

*Plus $2.00 for shipping. Offer open to residents of the U.S. and Canada only.
Canadian residents please call 1.800.481.9191 for pricing information.
If under 18, a parent or guardian must sign. Terms, prices and conditions subject to change. Subscription subject
to acceptance. Dorchester Publishing reserves the right to reject any order or cancel any subscription.

JOIN NOW!

Mark took a ragged breath. He looked at the wounded horse and felt like crying. He turned to Slim.

"You made a great ride," said Slim, but he didn't offer to shake hands. "You'll win the finals and the grand championship. You'll win yourself a farm . . . but," he said, his face inscrutable, "you mighty near killed one of the finest horses that ever came out of a chute."

"Me?" said Mark.

"If you'd put the bolt in that hasp like the judge told you," Slim said with finality, "the bull wouldn't have gotten out."

"What about the other men in the pens?"

"Who knows? The bull waited his chance . . . but if you had done your job instead of being sore at the judge over that calf roping, everything would have been all right."

They were walking along the fence, for another bucking horse had come out of the chute and was spraying an unlucky rider against the clouds.

"A horse that gave you a ride like that," Slim said disgustedly. "And you tried to kill him."

Mark looked away. He stared at the race track beyond the high fence. They were nearing the receiving pens.

"I used to think it was too much thinkin' about a dirty deal that made you act funny," said Slim, eyeing him distastefully, "but I see different now. It ain't somebody else that's eatin' you. It's *you*. You get mad and play the baby. You don't think." He hesitated. "I'll take that back. Maybe you do think. You took my advice once and did right well with it. I don't know. You ran out there to try to help that horse. Maybe 'way underneath you're all right, but you do some funny things." Slim drew a deep breath. "You come into rodeo," he said. "And I figger, when you come into rodeo and win rodeo prizes, you go by rodeo rules. Maybe that's what's the matter with you . . . you want to make up your own rules as you go along."

Mark eyed him and said slowly, thoughtfully: "Somebody else said that to me once."

"Somebody else was right. Somebody else knew what it took me four years to find out."

Mark didn't answer. It didn't seem there was any answer. He left Slim at the pens and cut across the track to the veterinary's barn. High Noon was strapped to his side on an inclined table. The veterinary was sewing up the gash in his side.

"How is he?" asked Mark.

The veterinary turned. He saw who Mark was and avoided his eyes. "He'll live, all right . . . but he won't do any more bucking this year."

Mark found the owner of the rodeo string. "What are you going to do with High Noon?" he asked.

The man pushed his tall hat back on his head. "I don't know. He won't be any good till next year . . . and I'm not sure of him, then. I've had horses hurt like that before, and it often ruins 'em as rodeo buckers. He might be all right. He might not. There's no guarantee even that he'll get well."

"I'll give you five hundred dollars for him," Mark said, "as he is."

The owner stared at Mark. "I reckon you want to make peace with yourself on account of leaving the bull out of that gate. The judge told me about that. Well, if that's the way you want to make it up, I got a notion to deal."

"I'll give you a check now."

"He's your horse, mister."

Mark spent the next hour hunting up a reliable place to care for High Noon until the tear was thoroughly healed. He paid in advance for three months. Then he went back to the headquarters building. He found out he had won over four thousand dollars all told, and, with the money he had, it was plenty to buy a farm.

The next morning the sun came down warm, promising an early spring and deep grass. Mark saddled the bay and hunted up Slim Junipher. "I'm leaving," Mark said.

Slim stared at him. "You're sittin' on top of the world. You could make twenty-five thousand this year."

"I might do the same as I did yesterday," Mark said. "I'm going home. I've got to find out about myself before I do anything more to hurt a man or an animal. To me that's more important than being grand champion cowboy of the world. I should have done it four summers ago, when you told me at Tulsa . . . but I didn't know what was eating on me then. I thought it was hate . . . but it was something else. I've got to find out if that something else is going to run me the rest of my life."

"When you think straight," Slim said finally, "you think *mighty* straight. Good luck."

Mark rode out of town and headed northwest. He wouldn't hurry. They wouldn't be plowing, up in his country, for quite a while yet. He could think things out. He knew what had gotten him into trouble over and over—he didn't like for people to tell him what to do—but he didn't know how to whip it. His father had sent him away so he could learn—but he hadn't learned. He'd turned right around and almost killed one of the finest horses that ever bucked—and maybe he'd do it again.

For nineteen hundred miles they jogged along, Mark trying to think things out but not getting beyond the place in his mind where he had been when he left San Antonio. Was it really Archie and his hatred of Archie that was eating on him all the time? He wondered. Was it resentment that lay deep under the surface? He couldn't tell. It was plain enough to him that Archie still was a thorn in his hide, but it didn't even seem quite right to blame Archie for a thing like leaving the gate unbolted at San Antonio.

Mark was still on that mental merry-go-'round when he rode into Selden, not really knowing what he was like inside, not knowing what to expect from himself when he reached home. And that was the way it was as he rode along the fence with Caroline. That was what stood between them, the uncertainty of his own behavior.

The gelding went almost to the creek, and swung right. Mark looked back. Caroline was sitting the stallion at the corner. Mark waved briefly. She answered slowly, uncertainly. He knew that she, too, was wondering what would happen.

He was already tense as he rounded the big willow tree. The farm was suddenly all laid out before him in the dusk; the small house he had been born in, the white picket fence that his father had kept painted in memory of his mother, the two rows of grapevines heavily loaded but not yet showing their dusty purple; the steel windmill pumping more and more slowly as the snow-cooled wind from the mountains began to lose its impetus toward sundown; the chicken yard filled with White Rocks that moved jerkily as they pecked at feed on the ground; a black-and-white cow with a new calf lying in the shade of the big oak tree on the high ground. He heard the ducks quacking down by the creek, and the big bullfrog he'd never been able to catch began booming in *basso profundo*. He smelled the heavy sweetness generated in a luxuriant land by the warmth of the sun. It always seemed to burst out of the ground as soon as the sun was low, to spread and settle over the earth when the wind quieted down.

All those things made Mark pause and breathe deeply. The sights and the sounds and the smells gave him an unutterable loneliness. This was his life. These things soaked into his bones, belonging there, but bringing him a sharp awareness of the reason he had come back—for all these agents of Nature were without doubts of themselves. They did what they were supposed to do and never questioned it. For a moment it struck Mark as ironic, for, of them all, he was a man and able to control his own destiny, and, of them all, he was unsure.

He rode into the farm yard slowly. Then he heard voices from beyond the barn.

His father's voice, coming first, seemed no different except that it was filled with weariness. "I told you to be sure to move those turkey houses."

Archie Warton's voice was deeper than Mark remembered it, but it was filled with juvenile contentiousness, as if he was anticipating a fuss with considerable pleasure. "We never move them that often down at our place."

"I'm tired of hearing what you do at your place," Mark's father said doggedly.

Mark got off the gelding. He tied the reins on a corral post. Then he walked around the corner of the barn. His father's back was toward him, but he could see the white wisp of hair standing up like a cowlick. His father was holding his hat in his hands. Archie Warton was leaning indolently against the barn, facing his father. Archie's hair was still black and slick, and his black eyes were still too shiny. Archie saw Mark and straightened. An oily smile spread over his face. "Will you look who's back!"

Mark's father whirled around. In his faded blue eyes there was first bafflement, but it softened after a moment and was replaced by that same inscrutable, guarded look that had been there when Mark had left. "Hello, Mark," he said.

"Hi, Dad."

"How's the boy?" asked Archie.

Mark looked at him. Archie had not changed, but Mark saw him through different eyes. Instead of seeing him as a contemporary who somehow always managed to sneak under the wire when there was trouble, he saw him as a boy grown up in years but small and mean and sniveling—puny was the word—in other ways. And for some reason, seeing him in this light, Mark did not feel the flood of resentment he had expected. Instead, he felt a surge of maturity. Abruptly but beyond question he knew that he himself was above that kind of thing and that he would always be above it.

He didn't answer Archie. He looked at his father and again at Archie. He noted Archie's still indolent posture against the side of the barn, and his father's words as he had come up. He didn't like Archie's too shiny eyes any more than he ever had, but now it was different. He felt no hate—only contempt. Archie was still playing at being a man, just as Mark had played at it four years before.

In that moment Mark knew what his father had meant by the coming home being more important than the leaving. And he knew what Slim had meant when he had said: "It's not somebody else eating on you. It's *you*!" He knew those things and felt a vast welling of understanding.

He looked coldly at Archie. He wanted no words with him. "Git!" he said.

Archie stared. He had started limply to offer his hand, but Mark stayed motionless and watched Archie steadily, feeling at a great distance. He noted the hand half raised—a hand still soft and smooth.

Archie hesitated. He licked his lips. His hand dropped back. He looked at Mark's father and met bleakness in the blue eyes. He looked at Mark and then away. "I'll be back after my wages," he muttered.

"Don't bother," Mark's father said. "I'll send them down."

Archie cut across to the creek. In a moment he was out of sight beyond the spire-like poplars.

The guarded look left Mark's father's face. His father grinned and held out his hand. Mark took it.

All the things that had been piled up ahead of him seemed suddenly to be pushed to one side. He shook hands hard.

"Glad to be back," he said.

"This is your country, Mark," his father said softly. "All you needed was to find it out." His blue eyes went all over Mark. Then he glanced at the poplars. He said as if proud: "You spoke with a voice of authority."

Mark said with distaste: "I've had enough of Archie's ways."

"You change," his father said, "more than things change here. But you can't see it in yourself. That's why it's so important to come back."

Mark murmured: "I know what you mean."

"Archie always did get you in trouble. It was good to see you take charge of him for a change."

"No," Mark said. "I realized when I looked at him ... Archie never got me in trouble. A man makes his own trouble."

He saw Archie walk out into the road and start down toward the Warton place. Archie stumbled a little as if he was walking self-consciously. Mark felt a little sorry for him.

Mark took a deep breath and looked back at his father. His father was looking at Mark's hands. Mark thought to look at them himself. They weren't smooth any longer. They were rough on the knuckles, and one thumb was cracked near the nail.

Mark turned with a new sense of power. He walked to the corner and looked up toward the Bird place. Caroline was at the corner of the apple orchard, on the big black. He waved. She waved back. Mark watched her turn the horse. Then he said to his father: "You'll be short of help. I better stay a while."

The white cowlick nodded with his father's head. His father put on his hat.

"O K," Mark said. "Where do you want those turkey pens?"

# The Man Who Had
# No Thumbs

Jonas Marson sat cross-legged and unmoving, watching juice drip from the haunch of mule meat and hearing it sizzle into the fire. He wore a big hat with the brim sagging at front and rear, and beneath it showed sandy hair, long and tangled and matted at the back where he lay on it while sleeping. His chin was covered with sandy whiskers stained brown from tobacco juice. Other men worked around him in the dark, sometimes visible in the blue glow of the burning cow chips. All were dressed in buckskin shirts and pants and moccasins, and they walked silently as if from long habit. Jonas paid no attention to them.

A man moved up to the fire and turned the meat with a scalping knife. He was tall and gangling and was a hunchback. His buckskin shirt was almost new, and a line of fifteen-inch fringes hung from the full length of each sleeve. He wiped the knife blade on his pants and grinned wolfishly at Marson. "You settin' there and thinkin' about all the years Nellie carried you across these here deserts?"

Marson's cold blue eyes rolled up to Hooker's whiskery face. "You always got your mind on women."

"I heard you say she was the best saddle mule in Mexico."

"She served her time," Marson said. "She couldn't carry a full load no more."

"That's the way you play, ain't it, Marson? Ev'r-body's got to carry his end . . . mules and all. That's why you're runnin' this outfit . . . you're smart."

Marson didn't answer.

Hooker looked into the darkness. "I'm thinkin' about Hobart."

"What about him?"

"What's he doin' out there in the desert some-where? When's he comin' back to get even?"

"What do you mean . . . get even?"

"I mean, well . . ."

"You mean you think I turned him over to the Apaches."

Hooker looked frightened. His head seemed to go down between his shoulders. "Not exactly . . ."

"If I did," Marson said, "he had it coming. He was a troublemaker. You heard him make threats to go to the governor at Chihuahua. I *had* to get rid of him."

"He said he was goin' to stop us killin'."

"You can't get scalps without killin'."

"Only thing is . . . them Delawares say he's a bad *hombre*."

Marson's lids half covered his eyes. "Go help the Dutchman side-hobble them mules."

Hooker slid the knife into the waistband of his pants and went hurriedly.

A second man came up—a heavy, round-barreled man with big shoulders. His eyes were jerky and nervous but flat as a snake's. He sat down a little way from Marson and stared into the desert darkness.

"We're gettin' mighty far into Chiricahua country."

"We come here to hunt Apaches, didn't we?"

Bixby frowned. "There ain't many of us, and there's thousands of Apaches."

"The Apaches kill for fun. We kill for money." Marson paused, rubbing the palms of his big hands on his greasy black pants. "The State of Chihuahua guarantees us a hundred *pesos* for every buck Apache scalp we bring back." His cold eyes gleamed. "That's better than gold mining . . . if we get where the Apaches are thick enough."

"What does the gover'ment want with scalps anyway?"

"Look!" Marson said impatiently. "The Apaches been depredatin' on the Mexicans for hundreds of years. Last year they practically come into Chihuahua itself and killed men and carried off women and kids. The Mexican *rurales* couldn't fight 'em, so they offered a bounty on 'em. That's where we come in. It's up to us," he said clumsily, "to save Mexico from the Apaches."

Bixby looked into the dark and frowned. "They say them Chiricahuas can take a sharp knife and make a man suffer more and live longer than any race that ever was."

Marson slapped his thigh impatiently. "Don't forget we got eighteen Delaware Indians with us . . . and the Delaware Indians are the best scouts and fighters in the United States."

"How many scalps did we get yesterday?"

Marson nodded at the tow sack hanging on a pole over the fire. "Fourteen . . . but six are squaws' and bring half price."

Bixby grunted. "Why was a little party like that away from the main tribe?"

"Hunting, I imagine. If it's going to be a cold winter, the game will be gettin' out of the mountains."

Bixby looked to the northwest and drew his thick shoulders up together. "I wouldn't want to put in a winter up there. Them are the wildest mountains in the world."

"We'll have to go up there after 'em unless we find some more hunting parties." Marson fixed his eyes on Bixby. "The next time I send you around to the other side, you cut 'em off or I'll cut your head off. You let a buck and two squaws get away yesterday. That's two hundred dollars."

Bixby's eyes jerked. He looked off into the dark. "There's a lot of coyotes out," he said.

"They ain't all coyotes."

"It sounds to me like there's more of 'em to the northwest."

"There are," said Marson, staring at the meat.

Bixby started up. "You reckon Chiricahuas . . . ?"

"Might be."

"We better . . ."

Marson reached out one big arm and slammed the man back to the ground. "Stay sat! There's more Delawares around them than they have any idea."

"They're comin' this way."

Marson stared at him contemptuously. "I wonder you ever had nerve enough to be a scalphunter."

"I've seen some bodies after the Apaches got through with 'em," Bixby muttered. "Ears cut off, eyes burned out, brains cut open." He shuddered. "You remember Jenkins? He was a scalphunter."

"Taught me my trade," said Marson. His big head raised sharply. Bixby saw the movement and stared into the darkness.

An Indian materialized on the other side of the fire. He was naked from the waist up, and the low blaze of the fire seemed to lose itself in the duskiness of his red skin before it reached his face. He wore heavy gold earrings, and his black hair, tied in two parts with buckskin thongs, hung behind his shoulders. The handle of a scalping knife protruded from the waistband of his elkskin pants, and a tomahawk was suspended at his side in a rawhide sling.

Marson's cold eyes moved upward. "*Kocu leu?*" he asked. "What is it?"

"*Pé shu-wún-uk,*" the Delaware said in his musical tongue. "A white man is coming."

"*Shin-gàh-leet?* Is he coming to fight?"

"*Túk-o.* No."

Marson's big head was motionless for a moment. He studied the deep shadows thrown upward across the bronze face by the blue glow from the fire. Then Marson said warily, as if to Bixby: "I don't know what a white man would be doing up here alone . . . but let him come." He nodded to the Delaware, who faded into the dark without a crunch of his moccasins on the hard sand.

"A white man," Marson repeated, and fingered the hilt of his big Bowie knife, with a blade eighteen inches long and three-eighths of an inch thick. He stared at the fire. "How would a white man get up here alone?"

"Maybe he was with a party that was attacked by the Apaches."

"There ain't no Mexican parties up in here," said Marson.

"Might be Americans."

"Too far south." Marson withdrew the knife and laid the end across his left forefinger. The finger was big, browned by the sun, and cracked at the joint. "This white man's a spy," he said.

Bixby watched the knife. Bixby's eyes looked hungry for a minute. Then he looked back into the dark.

Marson got up. He was as big standing as he looked sitting. He went to the fire, turned the meat spitted on the steel rod, and sliced off a big piece with one stroke of the Bowie knife. The meat dripped blood, but he held it in both hands and bit out a mouthful, his matted hair moving as a mass when he moved his head.

He was sitting down, still eating, when they first heard the steps. He quit eating and sat stone still, watching into the dark.

"I'll cover him for you," said Bixby.

"No need. If he makes a move, his back'll be full of Delaware arrows before he can draw a breath."

The crunch of dragging feet was clear in the

night. It came closer. Marson sat still, with the meat in one hand.

## II

A tall, slender man stumbled toward the fire. He, too, was dressed in buckskin that looked old and worn, and he had no hat. His whiskers were black and curled tightly against his chin. His moccasins were worn through, and his feet left blots of blood on the hardpacked surface of the sand.

Marson's eyes narrowed as he saw him, but Marson said nothing. The slender man drew himself up before the fire and fixed bloodshot eyes on Marson. His voice was a croak. "Water!" he said. "A little water."

Marson nodded. Bixby went to the wagon and came back with a horse's large intestine filled with water. He held it out to the stranger, who took a small sip to rinse his mouth. He waited a minute, then took a cautious drink of the greasy fluid. Finally he looked up at Marson. "I got away from the Chiricahuas four days ago," he said. "I been walkin' ever since."

"You're a liar," Marson said coldly. "You never escaped from no Apaches after this long."

The stranger took another short drink. "How do you think I got away?"

"You was sent," said Marson.

"Who'd send me?"

"The Apaches. They hate my guts and so do you. You turned coyote, Al Hobart, when you found out we was after scalps."

Hobart ripped open his worn buckskin shirt at

the front and showed a mass of white and red scars over his chest and stomach. "Does that look like something I asked for?" He took a final drink and handed the gut back to Bixby. "I didn't like it when you started scalping women and children. I said so."

"You run away," Marson accused, "to join the Apaches against my outfit."

Hobart was scornful. "You ever hear of anybody joining the Apaches?" The water had put life into him. He stood across the fire from Marson and asked: "Do I stay or do I light out for Chihuahua?"

"What do you want to go to Chihuahua for . . . to carry tales to the governor?"

"One of the first scalps you got *was* a Mexican," Hobart said calmly, but added: "I didn't *say* I wanted to cross two hundred kilometers of desert on foot . . . but I can."

Marson fingered the butt of his bowie knife, the handle of which was bound with the same fine brass wire as that on his shapeless hat, and studied it out.

Hobart didn't seem eager to go back into the desert alone. "If this had been a war party, the way you told me at first, I wouldn't have put up a holler," he said. "I don't like scalping the way you do it, but if I go back to Chihuahua, they might accuse me of deserting, and nobody would ever hire me as a guide again. On the other hand, you haven't got anybody else in your outfit that knows the Sierra Madres. That's why you been stalling out here in the *bolsón* so long with only a handful of scalps." He glanced at the almost empty tow sack.

Marson said finally: "If you can stay and mind your own business, I'll pay you the way I said."

"Including the last two months?"

Marson hesitated. Then his eyes were cold as he said: "Including all the time since we left Chihuahua." He paused. "But if you start talkin' against me again, I'll cut your head off myself the next time."

Al Hobart said slowly: "I never figured how the Chiricahuas got into camp that night through your Delawares . . . unless you told the Delawares to let 'em."

"Keep figurin'."

"And I never figured how they happened to pick on me that night and nobody else."

"Speak your piece," Marson growled.

"If I ever find out that was done by your orders, you'll *need* that big knife."

Marson grunted but said nothing.

Hobart glanced at the mule meat. "Got anything to cut that with?"

Marson nodded. Bixby tossed a knife at Hobart. The blade gleamed as it turned end over end. Hobart caught it by the handle. He wrapped four fingers around it and held the butt against the heel of his hand. Somewhat awkwardly he sliced off a piece of raw meat, wolfed it down, and tossed the knife back to Bixby.

He seemed to draw a breath of relief. "If you got a blanket," he said, "and a piece of buckskin for moccasins, I'll make out till morning."

"See Stephens at the wagon."

Hobart turned slowly.

"Wait a minute," Marson said.

The slender man stopped and looked at Marson.

Marson did not look up at him. "Search him," he said to Bixby. "See if he's got a knife of his own."

Bixby looked puzzled. Then he grinned. "*Seguro.*" He waddled over to Hobart and felt around his waistband, inside the buckskin shirt, under the tight-fitting deerskin leggings, inside the sleeves so worn that hardly any fringes were left on them. He stepped back, his eyes looking over the man. Hobart kept his brown eyes on him, unreadable; they might have meant anything.

Bixby shook his head. "Nothin' on him."

"There could be something inside of him," Marson said, running big fingers through his tangled whiskers, "but there'll be a chance to find that out later on.

Hobart limped into the darkness.

Bixby let out his breath. "So he's back."

"Watch him," Marson said, and this time he didn't sound so sure of himself. "That Hobart was captured by the Comanches when he was a pup. They raised him, and he learned all their tricks and some of his own. He's worse than any Apache that ever lived."

Bixby's flat eyes fastened on Marson. "He's been gone two months, hasn't he?"

"Yeah."

"A man can't live in the desert by himself for two months, can he?"

"Not the way I figger."

Bixby said: "The muscles on his waist are hard. He ain't starved."

Marson looked up, his eyes alive for the first time. "Like I said, keep an eye on him. I could turn him out, but I'd rather have him in my sight. Whatever he's up to, I'll be able to put my hands on him."

Bixby took a deep breath. He got up and went to the fire. He cut off a chunk of meat and came back with it in his hands. "Nellie don't look as tough as I calc'lated." He took a bite, and then looked up. His mouth was full, and his bright, beady eyes watched Marson. "You notice . . . somethin' happened to his thumbs?"

"He hasn't got any," said Marson.

Bixby frowned. "Wonder what happened."

Marson got up—a ponderous man who yet moved like a jaguar. "Whatever it was, he had it comin'."

"You ain't curious about how?"

Marson took a deep breath that seemed to fill out his belly. "I don't have to worry about Hobart no more. A man can't cock a pistol without a thumb."

*III*

The camp was moving the next morning before daylight. Hobart led off toward the foothills of the towering Sierra Madres. Then came Marson on his mule, with Hooker beside him, and two more hunters behind them. The bushy-whiskered Stephens drove the wagon, followed by Bixby and three others. The Delawares fanned far out from the column in all directions; their job was to locate game, to forestall attacks, and to find parties of Indians that could be scalped.

They crossed open desert plains, mesas lightly timbered with scrub oak, and the great prairie began to slope up. It rose gradually at first, then began to dip and rise, and finally there were steep-sided washes that they had to go around. On the fifth day they went up a narrow cañon, with not even room to turn on the trail, and pines and junipers began to dot the steep mountainsides. Then the mountains seemed to close in on them, with mile-high cliffs, huge granite blocks dumped end on end and left that way, wild white-water torrents pouring through bottomless cañons, and ragged rocky steps that mounted endlessly to the blue sky. Behind them, the sky was brassy and the sun like a leaping flame, but Marson drove the mule train on to the northwest.

Great outcroppings of black granite appeared, and each time they had to find a way upward over the rock. Each time the air got thinner. The ground became harder, and they had to shoe the mules. Small cedars, twisted into grotesque shapes by the fantastically cold and violent winter winds of the Sierra Madres, grew around the outcroppings, and presently these gave way to pines and the great spruce.

It seemed that the higher they went and the deeper they penetrated the savage country, the deeper grew the antagonism between Marson and Hobart. Even the Delawares knew it was there. And if any man had a leaning one way or the other— which was doubtful—he kept it to himself. This was a fight between Marson and Hobart. Eventually it would erupt, and probably Hobart would be killed; then the business of scalphunting would be resumed.

Scalps had not been plentiful. They had not, in fact, found a single Apache since that night when Hobart had appeared out of the desert. There were no more small hunting parties to be massacred, and grumbling began to be evident in the muttered tones of the scalphunters as they went to hunt deer or as they took guard duty over the mules at night. The Delawares came and went, silently, more unseen than seen. They found some game, but no Chiricahuas. The mules were gaunt; the men lost weight; even Marson sloughed off some meat, but it only made him look harder and tougher.

Marson called Hobart one day. "Where's the Apaches?"

Hobart took his time answering. He looked at the low, thin cloud bank beyond the mountains. A few great cranes were following a cañon toward the south. Hobart said finally: "On up . . . is my guess."

Marson growled: "How high do these damn' mountains go?"

"To the top."

Marson stared at him. "There's villages up in here. Where are they?"

"Can't your Delawares find them?"

Marson swelled up. "If you want your cut of the profits, you'd better come through." His eyes narrowed as if he had had a shrewd thought. "You don't owe them Chiricahuas anything, do you, that you have to protect them?"

"They can protect themselves up here," Hobart said, "if they use any sense at all."

"They don't."

"No," said Hobart. "They don't murder for money."

Marson fingered his bowie knife. "Why are you so squeamish? They said in Chihuahua you'd raised more scalps than any man in Mexico."

Hobart drew himself up, lean and tough and dangerous. "I've raised hair," he said, "and I would have come on a war party. But you know enough about me to know I wouldn't like scalping for money. That's why you got me drunk and shanghaied me. You'll pay for that, Marson. I've done a lot of things I'm not proud of, and mostly I've filled up on mescal and forgotten 'em, but this one I don't forget. I didn't know you were out to exterminate the Apache nation by killing off squaws and kids."

Marson said: "You came back fast enough."

"When a man needs water, he can't worry about other things. Besides, you owed me money."

"Where's the Apache towns?" Marson insisted.

Hobart shrugged. "They're here one day, somewhere else the next. There's only one town in this part of the mountains that stays put and that's Santa Margarita, over the hump."

"Indians there?"

Hobart shook his head. "All Mexicans . . . living on top of a silver mine . . . the richest mine on earth."

Marson's cold eyes gleamed. "Is that Tayopa?"

Hobart watched him. "Who knows?"

"How do they stand off the Indians?"

The scalphunters stood around them now on the windswept shelf of rock—Bixby, Hooker, Stephens, and the others, all gaunt, unshaved, hard-eyed killers—and Hobart looked around as if amused. "The Indians don't fight very systematically unless they're mad. The Mexicans in Santa Margarita don't do anything to make them mad." Hobart swept the audience with his eyes, then faced Marson again. "They don't murder for twenty-five *pesos* a head, and women about to have babies for seventy-five."

"What are you talkin' about?" growled Marson.

"I figgered it was the last straw when you cut open a dead Indian squaw so you could scalp the baby she was carryin'."

Marson's face began to turn dark. The circle around them stretched out a little. "I could make you eat what you just said."

"Maybe," said Hobart, watching him.

"But I need you. I'm gonna keep you working for me like you agreed, because you're the only one who knows these mountains. Then, when we come back, I'm gonna cut your head off and feed it to the coyotes."

"Good enough," Hobart said.

He waited until Marson turned away. Then he resumed his way up the endless slope.

## IV

It was a world above a world up here—wild, forbidding, friendless, but one evening Hobart came into camp with a dressed-out bear carcass on his back. He said nothing, but dropped it before the fire, and left.

Bixby's flat eyes followed him until he disappeared among the rocks. "How'd he get that critter?" asked Bixby. "He hasn't got a pistol, and he couldn't shoot one if he did."

Marson turned the carcass with his moccasin. "He's got a knife," he said harshly.

So the antagonism between the two men grew and festered and spread like maggots in a dead horse as the company got higher into the mountains. Up there the wind was always like a gale, and it was always cold, but Hobart, at Marson's order, led up and up.

Within a week Marson called Hobart to the fire. It was night, and the wind was biting cold. It whistled through the rocks until even the mules turned tail to it.

"Where's Santa Margarita?"

Hobart's eyelids dropped a little. "I told you that's a Mexican town," he said.

"I ast you where it is."

"Are you aimin' to scalp Mexicans now?"

Marson looked at him with hatred. "I'm runnin' this company. Where's Santa Margarita?"

"I'll show you, if you promise not to massacre the Mexicans for their scalps."

Marson was suddenly on his feet. He had moved astonishingly fast for a big man. And his Bowie knife, as big as a sword, was in his hands. "You lead the way," he said harshly, "or I'll . . ."

"Cut my head off," Hobart said.

Marson's leathery face began to turn black.

Hobart suddenly broke and backed away.

Marson drew a great breath and thrust the knife back in its holster. "Dirty mare-suckin' coward!" he growled.

Hooker grinned his wolfish grin. "You don't need

to be scared of him," he said. "He can't shoot, and he can't knife fight. He's got no thumbs."

Bixby said: "He's never told how he lost them thumbs, did he?"

Marson glanced coldly at him. "I don't care how he lost his thumbs," he said finally.

"Naw," said Hooker. "All you want is to see him lose his head." Hooker frowned, puzzled. "I never figgered Hobart would take a dare like that."

Marson looked into the darkness at the spot where he had last seen Hobart. "Every man," he said, "comes to a place where he has to eat his own spit." But his voice did not carry the assurance that his words seemed to indicate.

The next morning, when the Delawares reported there still was no fresh Apache sign, Al Hobart led the company up over a spur to the southwest. There had been a spit of snow up there the night before, and Bixby shivered as they faced the sweeping wind. "I don't like none of this," he grumbled. "Hobart rides up there out of sight, and he's the only one knows anything about the country."

"He'll take us where we want to go," said Marson. "He knows what'll happen to him if he don't."

Their supplies gave out, and they began to kill mules of necessity. The weaker ones went first. One of the scalphunters, beating a balky mule over the head with a bridle, slipped on a crumbly shelf of rock and dropped eight hundred feet to the bottom of a cañon. They didn't bother to go after his body. So now there were nine white men left, and the mule meat stretched further. Marson did not feed it to the Delawares. "They're Injuns," he said. "They don't have to be fed."

They saw Hobart twice a day—in the morning before daylight and at night after dark, when he came to the fire to claim his piece of mule meat.

Marson objected one day. "You don't need any of my meat. You can find your own."

For perhaps the first time a glint appeared in Hobart's eyes. "The deal was for found," he said. He looked at Marson, and there was a hint of a smile on his lean and wind-weathered face. "The more I eat," he said, "the less you have."

They heard the bells of Santa Margarita one clear morning before the wind rose. They couldn't see the village, but Hobart led them onto a perilous trail down a sheer cañon wall, twelve hundred feet to the bottom, and they came out in a grassy valley a couple of hundred *varas* wide, with a twenty-foot-wide stream roaring through the middle of it.

"It don't look safe to me," said Bixby, his eyes darting up and up to the top. "A man couldn't get out of here nohow."

"We didn't come to run," Marson reminded him. "We come for scalps . . . and maybe something else."

Hooker, his awkward knees sticking out on both sides of his saddle mule, grinned. "You figure there's any women at this here town?"

"There's always women," Marson said coldly.

They could see Hobart for a while, riding far ahead down the cañon, keeping in touch with them through the Delawares, but presently he was gone.

Later they turned up a second cañon and began to climb again. At the end of the second day they reached the top of the ridge, and the next morning again they heard the bells.

Marson said to Hobart: "We heard them bells two days ago. You leadin' us in a circle?"

Hobart had seemed more and more sure of himself as they had come higher and deeper into the mountains. Now he answered: "What difference does it make . . . as long as you get there?"

"We can't eat mule meat forever."

That wasn't the answer Marson would have liked to make, but it was worrying him some, getting so far into the mountains. Nine men weren't a very big party, and you had to knock off one for Hobart; he'd never fight with the rest of them; he was too much Indian. The Delawares were Indians, and a man never knew what an Indian was thinking or what he would do. On the other hand, it was a long way back, and their tow sack had only a few scalps in the bottom instead of bulging full as Marson had envisioned it. He maintained contact with Hobart through the Delawares, and kept the company going forward.

Santa Margarita was a tiny Mexican village perched on a narrow shelf of black rock halfway down a mountainside. Marson and Bixby and Hooker stood on a cliff so high they could hardly see the bottom and studied the town, a league away across the cañon and two thousand *varas* lower. It was late evening. From where they watched, they could see the blazing sun setting behind higher and still more rugged peaks covered with new snow. But down below them the grass and the trees were green, and the dull waxy green of orange leaves was plain in the soft light. Thin columns of fragrant cedarwood smoke rose straight into the air and then mingled into a single column before it reached the chill torrent of air sweeping over the mountain.

"There's the church," Marson said with satisfaction.

Bixby said: " 'Bout twenty houses. You reckon it's worth it?"

Marson's eyes were narrow. "They're sittin' on top of a silver mine. Hobart said so." Marson grunted with satisfaction. "Hobart never realized he told me that."

"You reckon they've got any silver?"

"Couldn't help it. They've been there for hundreds of years, diggin' it up. There's prob'ly tons of the stuff in that old church."

"Do we think we ought to fight the church?" asked Hooker.

Marson said nastily: "Them priests bleed like anybody else."

"I ain't worried about the church," said Bixby, scanning the trail on the opposite side of the cañon. "You seen Hobart today?"

Marson looked up quickly. "What could he do?"

"He could warn 'em down there."

"My Delawares been watchin' every move he makes. They got orders to knife him if he tries to signal."

"And he hasn't?"

"I can guarantee that."

Bixby nodded slowly. "Only thing is . . . it don't seem right for him to give up so easy."

"He knows when he's licked. He can't fight anyway. He hasn't got any thumbs."

Bixby turned toward him. He might have been about to say something, but, if so, he changed his mind. He turned back to Santa Margarita. "There's people down there."

"Twenty houses . . . maybe sixty, eighty scalps." His eyes gleamed. "Maybe five thousand dollars."

"There'll be women," said Hooker, grinning.

Marson spoke slowly. "There'll be silver, too . . . enough to go where a man wants to go. I'll take my women in Mexico City . . . maybe even in Paris." He drew a deep breath.

Hooker was watching the village again. "No sense in waitin' that long," he said.

The yapping of dogs came to them on the wind. "There'll be a moon tonight," said Marson. "As soon as it comes up, we'll cross the cañon and go down the trail. You take four men and get on the other side. We'll split the Delawares between us. We'll get the lay of things, and I figure by two, three o'clock in the morning we'll attack." The first clear peal of the church bell came to them, mellow, measured, serene. "They'll all be through makin' love by that time, and we'll have the mountains to ourselves."

"What about the priest?"

"His scalp's worth a hundred dollars," Marson said coldly.

"What if the governor at Chihuahua . . . ?"

"How can he tell the difference between an Apache and a Mexican? They're both brown skins. They both got straight black hair. The main thing is . . . kill everyone. If one gets away, he can tell."

"They won't get away from me," Bixby promised.

Hooker grinned, thinking his own thoughts.

A half hour later Marson told Hobart what he wanted. Hobart asked: "Are you going to scalp these Mexicans?"

"Don't worry about what I'm gonna do. Just lead us right or you'll die with this knife in your jugular vein."

Hobart's lips parted. He closed them. He looked down at his thumbless hands. Finally his eyes left Marson. He looked at the village below, which now was in deep shadow and would have been indistinguishable except for the tiny yellow lights of deer-fat candles. Hobart's hand went to his waist, but finally he said: "The Mexican governor will have your head for a stunt like this, Marson."

The big man laughed. "If he could get my head, he wouldn't have sent me after Apaches."

The lights of Santa Margarita went out early, but the scalphunters, traveling in a tight group except for the Delawares, were already across the chasm, and sometime after midnight they were within shouting distance of the small cluster of adobe huts. Marson stopped to repair a broken cinch strap with a fine brass wire.

"Go 'way around," he told Bixby. "Look out for the dogs. Give me an owl hoot three times when you're ready."

Bixby and his four men left the trail, going above the village to avoid the rising air currents. Four men went with him, each armed with two six-shooters and at least two knives, plus whatever personal weapon each man preferred.

Marson counted noses. He had three men at his

back and Hobart at his side. The Delawares spread out and lost themselves on the mountainside. When the attack started, the Delawares would swarm over the village from all sides.

They waited, each man with his hand on his mule's nose. Finally, across the night wind, came the hoot of an owl, echoing eerily up the cañon. It came again, and a third time. Marson growled— "No prisoners!"—and swung into the saddle. He beat the mule into a gallop. In the darkness he could hear the Delawares closing in at both sides. He kept to the trail.

They charged into the little area that held the town. The Delawares joined in with their blood-chilling war cry. Bixby hammered on a door with the butt of a revolver. "*Abre la puerta in nombre del rey!* Open up, in the name of the king!"

A door opened. A shot sounded. A groan. The door crashed in. Its rawhide hinges shrieked as they gave away. A woman screamed, and there was another shot. Then children shrieked, and there was silence for an instant.

By that time the moonlit town was filled with fighting figures. The scalphunters swung knives and clubs like fiends: they fired only when they had to. Marson himself rode into the church on his mule and cut off the priest's head with his big knife, swung like a guillotine.

The mountainside swelled with the whoops of the Delawares, the yells of the hunters, the pleas of the cornered, and the curses of the dying.

Hobart rode alongside Marson. He took no part in the killing, but Marson didn't care. Marson was drunk now on blood and carnage, and, when it was over, he would wind it up by taking care of Hobart. Nobody would ever know the difference in this excitement.

Hooker was down, scalping bodies. He yanked off a long, black-haired scalp with a loud pop, and held it up in the moonlight. "There's women here!" he screamed at Marson.

Marson pulled up his mule and looked around. All over town, men were on the ground, ripping off scalps. Marson started to dismount. Hobart dismounted with him, and Marson gripped his Bowie knife and started around the rump of the mule. But a new sound came on the night air.

*"Wah-wah-wah-wahwah-ee-yah . . . WA-A-A-AH!"*

Marson froze in his tracks. "Apaches!" he said hoarsely.

Hobart was coming at him then. The man's slender face was grim in the moonlight, and his eyes were filled with the glitter of revenge. The long fingers of his right hand were wrapped around the butt of a scalping-knife, holding it against the heel of his hand. The blade stood at an awkward angle, but there was no mistaking that it could kill.

Marson was stunned for a moment. Then, as Hobart reached him, he swung the big knife like a sword. Hobart swung to one side. The heavy blade cut into Marson's own saddle.

Flames roared up from the church as the Chiricahuas swept down into the town. Marson fired a six-shooter with his left hand. He had the satisfaction of seeing blood spread over Hobart's face. The man's left cheekbone was plainly missing in the light of the fire, and blood was pumping out of the open flesh. But Hobart closed in with the long, thin-bladed knife. Against the cracking of the fire and the yells of the Chiricahuas, there was sudden silence from the scalphunters. In the red glow of the fire, Hobart's face didn't change. His knife slid in between Marson's ribs. His hand without a thumb threw Marson's arm to one side, his long fingers wrapped around Marson's wrist.

Marson cut at him savagely with the big knife, but Hobart closed in. His knife was out of Marson's ribs and in again.

Marson pushed him back with all his weight. Hobart stumbled. Marson fired again with the six-shooter, and saw Hobart jerk when the ball hit him. But Hobart came up under Marson's bowie knife. The thin blade of Hobart's knife went through Marson's right wrist. The bowie knife fell from Marson's fingers while Hobart rolled into him and kept the pistol arm flung wide. The man was slippery as an eel. Marson couldn't get hold of him, and he couldn't shoot. He sank his teeth in the back of Hobart's neck. Hobart raised hard and butted him in the face. Marson's knife gleamed redly on the ground in the light of the burning church. Hobart backed away for an instant. Marson shook his big head to get his wits back. He roared at Hobart with both arms wide, but the slender man stepped back as Marson leaped. He swung one foot and kicked Marson under the chin as he fell. He took the pistol. A rawhide thong slipped around Marson's neck. He saw Hobart pick up his big knife. Then he lost consciousness.

\* \* \*

When he came to, he felt as if all the fiends of hell were crawling up and down his backbone. He started to his feet, but couldn't move. He tried to roar, but found his tongue was split and swollen. He got his eyes open.

He was naked, lying on his face. Hobart sat cross-legged at one side, holding a knife in his four-fingered hand. An Apache with a red head-band sat on the other. Marson felt movement over his face and tried to brush it off, but his hands were staked down.

He saw the ants crawling over him from the hill beneath his belly. He felt their sharp pincers in his flesh, and suddenly he screamed. The screaming opened the cuts in his tongue and filled his mouth with blood. He coughed it out, and lay there panting.

The sun came down on his back like a hot iron. The blood made his mouth and throat as dry as old wood.

The Apache looked at Hobart. *"Besh?"* he asked. "Knife?"

Hobart nodded slowly. The Apache took a knife from the deerskin pocket below his knee and went to work on Marson's back. Marson fainted when the Indian flayed back a piece of skin as big as his hand, and the ants began to crawl over it.

Marson regained consciousness late that night. Hobart was still sitting there. Marson's voice was a croak. "I'll give you anything you want, if you'll let me up."

Hobart pointed to the small group of low-thatched *jacales* spread out under red-barked, wild cotton trees. "You were lookin' for a Chiricahua camp. This is it." He nodded at the ring of beady-eyed Indians, with moccasins turned up at the toes, who now surrounded them. "They would kill me if I interfered with their fun. Anyway, what does it matter? You'll be dead only once."

"They're fiends," Marson said hoarsely.

"Like you said . . . they kill for fun. They also kill for revenge. If they happen to admire you, they'll kill you without marking up your body." Hobart paused. "I don't think your body will be recognizable, Marson. You had some Apache scalps in your tow sack."

"You set them on us," said Marson. "How?"

"You sent word to the Chiricahuas to come and get me. You gave them the brass wire to hang me up by my thumbs. I got poisoning in my thumbs, but I didn't die. After five days in the sun, they cut me down. My thumbs were both cut to the bone by that fine wire, and gangrene was starting. I borrowed a knife and cut off both of them. They were impressed, Marson, and I made a deal with them. If they'd let me go, I'd bring you to them. That's why I came back."

"How did they know? The Delawares were watchin' you every minute. You never had any contact with the Chiricahuas."

"The Delawares are mighty good scouts," said Hobart, "but they're no match for the Chiricahuas in their own country. When the Chiricahuas know you're in the mountains, they can watch you for weeks, and you'll never know it. And they aren't dumb, Marson. I told them I'd take you to Santa Margarita, and they could nail you there. So they just watched and waited."

The Apache with the knife came toward them. Marson tried to scream again when the knife blade started to work on his back, but his tongue was too swollen. He felt the ants crawling into his raw flesh, and opened his eyes. Hobart was toying with the big bowie knife, hefting it with the four fingers of his right hand, but Marson didn't have time to hope.

A spasm of pain went through him, and he twisted against the rawhide ropes that only became tighter.

Marson was a big man, and he was hard. But not hard enough. The crags along the Rio Mayo rang with his screams for three days before the Apaches finished with him. It would have been longer, but even the Apaches couldn't keep him alive forever.

# The Fighting Road

Pop Gregory rode his bedroll in a corner of the jolting wagon, trying to think. He wished they hadn't gotten off to such a bad start. He watched his tall son and then said wistfully: "Maybe you'll like logging in Oregon."

The boy made an impatient quirk with his mouth and looked away. Then the rear wheels hit a big root in the tote road and the wagon lurched. Pop Gregory's son, caught off balance, went flat on his face.

Pop waited, but as soon as the boy was up, Pop went on: "A man has to have the real stuff in him to log out here." He had meant it to be proud, but it turned out to be defensive.

The boy looked at Pop finally. The boy was a tall, young man, light of hair and fair of face, broad in the shoulders and slim in the waist. For eighteen he was quite a man, but he showed the sharp cynicism of youth when he said: "That's what Mother always said when you were gone all winter."

Pop was glad there wasn't anybody else in the back end of the wagon. He looked toward the front. He didn't think the driver could hear them. Pop's thin eyebrows were twisted in hurt and confusion. He said cautiously: "With your mother just gone and all, I thought we'd come out here and work together and be pals, like." It sounded silly, coming from a tough old logger, but he was glad he'd said it. "I never had much time to know you, with logging all winter in the woods and working downriver on a sawmill in the summer." He added plaintively: "I kind of thought we'd get better acquainted."

The boy turned on him. "You let me grow up without a father, and now you want to step in and take over." Suddenly the pent-up bitterness and the hurt of a disillusioned boy came pouring out in words. "All those years," he said, a little over-dramatically, "I saw you three or four weeks a year, and, when I did, you spent all your time telling me about logging . . . mostly about fighting. I thought that was all you ever did in the woods in the winter time . . . was fight."

Pop said guiltily: "I tried to entertain you."

"Maybe you did," said the boy. "And maybe it gave me some wrong ideas. The kids at school teased me because my father was always gone, so I did what I thought you would have done . . . I licked hell out of 'em."

He said it defiantly, and Pop knew it was because the boy never before had used profanity in front of him, and Pop knew, too, the depth of the boy's rebellion and hurt. Pop should not have allowed that word to pass unchallenged, but he did, because there was nothing else he could do.

"By the time I was in the ninth grade," continued the boy, "I had licked every kid in *all* the grades . . . big and little. I made 'em say 'sir' to me . . . just the way I figured you made the lumberjacks do to you."

"No logger ever says 'sir,'" Pop said.

"Not to *you*," said the boy.

"Well . . . ?"

"I came out here with you expecting to see something like . . . well, a giant, almost, pushing men over with both hands if they didn't bow to him. And what did I see when I got to Lodgepole?"

Pop looked away.

The boy said sadly: "Somehow I never had looked at you straight. I always saw you in my mind, and you were always the biggest and toughest man in the woods . . . but this morning I found out. You're too small, and you're too old. Nobody will even fight you."

"I tried to show you . . . ," Pop began miserably.

"Yeah," said the boy. "You tried to pick a fight with Black Bill Sullivan, and he laughed at you and pushed you in the face and sat you down in the mud. I was ashamed. He didn't even take you seriously enough to hit you."

"Well," said Pop, trying desperately to find a way out, "I . . . I'm not a troublemaker. Everybody knows that. I've fought, all right . . . plenty. But not without reason. And maybe I am a little older. I'm old enough to have some sense, maybe."

"It doesn't cut any ice with me," the boy declared. "You raised me on fight stories, and I've grown up fighting. I came up here to fight. If you can't hold up your end, I'll hold up both ends. I'll lick every man in the woods by myself."

"You can't do that," Pop said quickly. "These men fight differently. They fight to kill or cripple."

"I can learn how to do that."

Pop swallowed. It was even more serious than he had realized. He looked at the boy and said slowly: "That's no way to start out in life. If you start doing that, you'll have to keep on the rest of your life. They'll never leave you alone, because there'll always be somebody younger and stronger, and, if you get started that way, you'll never be able to quit. Your pride won't let you . . . until someday you'll wind up with a butcher knife through your collarbone." He shook his head slowly. "That's the wrong way to start out in the woods, Sonny. There's plenty of fighting without looking for it."

"I was raised on fighting," the boy said stubbornly, "and, since I've got to do it all for both of us, I've got to get busy." He added sharply: "And whatever you do, don't call me 'Sonny' out here. I don't want to start out with *that* handicap."

Pop had a bad taste in his mouth. He worked his jaws for a moment, and then, realizing that was the mark of an old man, he stopped and looked down at his thumb. He'd never dreamed he would be faced with a problem like this almost before he got his breath. His son was big and strong and quick and would make a good logger, and he didn't want him to take the fighting road. Even if he should learn the dirty tricks fast and manage to stay alive, he'd never have a friend, that way. A man could fight, of course—a man had to fight sometimes, but for a man to go into the woods with a chip on his shoulder—that was suicide. Pop felt low.

Pretty soon he tried again. "This first camp up on Pine Mountain," he said, "will be the superintendent's office. We'll get our assignments there. They'll have three or four crews in our division this year, but I'll ask Fred to put you in with my bunch. I wouldn't want you to start out under a foreman like Black Bill."

The boy made an effort to be polite. The effort was obvious. "Who's foreman of the crew you'll be in?"

Pop's chest swelled. "Mike Brady," he said, "the cat-footedest river pig that ever wore stagged pants in icy water." He beamed at the boy.

But his son sighed noisily and looked away. "All right," he asked resignedly, "what's so wonderful about Mike Brady?"

For an instant it got Pop. He felt like batting his son over the head. But he got control of himself. After all, the boy had been without a father all his life. Pop swallowed and started with as much renewed enthusiasm as he could: "Mike's bunch can cut more logs than any crew west of Michigan."

The wagon driver, a whisker-faced man, looked back over his shoulder. "I hear Black Bill has licked him for three straight summers, down at Lodgepole."

Pop's lips compressed. Then he said: "Black Bill is older and bigger. Mike is still puttin' on weight." But he saw the quick expression on his son's face, and for the first time he began to feel hopelessness. His whole idea was toppling like an undercut redwood.

For the first time now he realized how much he had been depending on Mike Brady, for in Pop's mind Mike was a man in every sense of the word, and Mike respected Pop. So Pop had figured the boy would adopt Mike as his personal hero, as did everybody else in Mike Brady's crew, and he would see Mike's attitude toward Pop, and his own attitude would change. For Pop wasn't deluding himself. His son had little for him right now but contempt. And Pop, sitting there on his bedroll, moving with the jouncing wagon, watching his son from the corner of his eye, knew one thing for sure: although he didn't like the contempt, he could stand it; the thing that hurt was that his son should grow up to be a bully. It was something that he could not endure—but he might have to.

The superintendent's camp was made up of three log buildings in a clearing, and the area that November afternoon was filled with several hundred men—some sitting on stumps, whittling, some milling around, some standing in groups.

Pop stood up in the wagon and looked around. When the wagon stopped, Pop, with his bedroll under one arm, jumped off. The boy followed him. Pop, grim-faced, pushed his way into a crowd.

In a circle of men, two big men were facing each other. One had his back toward them, and facing him was a man with a black beard. He was six feet two and built like an ox. He was grinning but without humor; his face seemed set in that expression, but his eyes were bold and hard. He said: "It was one of your logs that caused the big jam this side of Glacier Lake this summer."

Mike Brady said slowly—"You're wrong."—and Pop didn't like the sound of it, for he knew Mike was trying to evade a fight.

Black Bill persisted. "It was a redwood butt, and it had your end marks on it."

"I don't believe it," said Mike, "but what difference does it make now?"

Bill pushed forward. "You don't believe it? What do you aim to do about it?"

Mike's voice was tight when he answered: "Nothing . . . now."

Their faces were less than a foot apart. Mike didn't move back. Black Bill said goadingly: "After that stomping I gave you in Lodgepole last July, maybe you don't like to fight no more."

The muscles hardened at the corners of Mike's jaws, but he held his voice level. "I don't fight in the woods. This is a place to work." His lips were open to say more, but he closed them. He looked Black Bill in the eye and then turned and walked away, pushing through the crowd of muttering men.

Pop hurried after him. He grabbed his big arm and said eagerly: "Hi, Mike."

Mike turned to look at him. Mike's face was grim. He didn't seem to see Pop right away. He looked over Pop's head toward Bill Sullivan. Then he looked back at Pop again, and finally he seemed to get hold of himself. His mouth broke into a smile that finally spread over his face. He said: "Pop! How are you?"

Pop felt a warm glow all over. He looked proudly at Mike's six feet one and his hundred and ninety-five pounds. He took in the big shoulders and arms, the deep chest and the narrow waist. He said: "Mike, I want you to meet my boy. He's going to work this winter. Think we can get him in your crew?"

Mike's blue eyes took in the boy, and Pop watched anxiously. He was relieved, when Mike's eyes warmed, and Mike stuck out a huge hand. "I think we can fix it up. How old are you, sonny?"

Pop caught his breath. The boy stiffened for a moment, but he shook hands with Mike. "Eighteen," he said. He looked back deliberately at Black Bill. Then he turned slowly and said to Mike: "I thought you were going to fight."

Mike took it the way the boy intended it. They were almost the same height, but the way Mike looked at him, it didn't seem so. He said harshly: "You'll see plenty of fighting this winter . . . but not in my crew until we get to Lodgepole next summer, and the drive is over. If you're going to be in my crew, sonny, you'll have to work."

Pop was sweating when he took the boy to the superintendent's office. Just before they went inside he tried to explain: "There's a lot more things make a good foreman than fighting."

The boy answered sarcastically: "Mike Brady must have all the other things."

Pop was disheartened when he talked it over with Mike that evening. "He always begged me to tell him stories about fighting, and maybe I laid it on a little," he confessed.

Mike agreed. "He's got a one-track mind about fighting."

Pop shook his gray head. "He's at a crisis in his life, Mike. What he does for the next year will probably decide what he will do the rest of his life."

"Maybe so," said Mike.

"He doesn't respect me, and somehow everything else is wrong, too."

"He's disappointed," said Mike. "He built you up as a hero in his mind, and it's a shock to realize maybe he overdid it a little. But he'll get over that. A boy naturally leans toward his dad. Sometimes it takes a jar to bring it out."

"The only thing that would change him," said Pop gloomily, "is for me to lick somebody . . . but there ain't nobody in camp that would even fight me, and he's too young to understand why. I was hoping he'd go for you and that would . . ."

Mike was whittling out a toothpick. "You're on the wrong track there, Pop. Only one person in the world can make somebody else respect you . . . and that's Pop Gregory."

Pop was silent for a moment. "It don't sound so good," he said at last.

He was depressed when Mike agreed with him. "I guess you can't force it, Pop," he said gently. "It might only turn out worse. Better let nature take its course."

It seemed to jerk everything out from under Pop. There he was, watching his big, young son take the wrong road, and there wasn't a thing he could do about it.

Presently he said: "What's eating on Black Bill today?"

Mike whittled. "Fred Canary is going to the home office after this winter, and Bill wants to be superintendent of the Lodgepole Division. He's trying to eliminate everybody else by scaring them to death."

Pop snorted. "This would be one hell of a place to work if he was superintendent. But why didn't you take him on? You woulda whipped him this summer if you hadn't slipped in the mud."

Mike's fingers touched the side of his face, where there was a long, white scar. "Yes," he said finally, "but then there would be an outbreak of fighting all over camp. If the foremen fight, the men will fight. It would have cost the company a million feet of logs before the winter is over. I'm here to cut logs." He made a vicious slash with his jackknife and cut the inch-thick limb in two pieces. "Sometimes," he said, getting up, "it's harder not to fight than it is to fight. I did the way I thought was right."

When morning came and the work lists were posted, Pop Gregory got a blow, for his boy's name was listed with Bill Sullivan's outfit. Pop read it and choked. Then he was indignant. He turned to the boy and said: "What's the matter with that Fred Canary? I'll see him and get that straightened out. I've been working for him for fifteen years. I've got some rights."

But the boy looked down at his father, and the way he did it made Pop suddenly shrink. The boy said: "I asked for Black Bill's crew. I don't want to be coddled. I want to grow up with *men*."

So the boy followed Black Bill's wanigan up Crooked River, while Pop, eating his heart out in a way that he had never imagined anybody but a weakling would do, went with Mike Brady up Rock River.

Mike tried once to console him. "If the kid's got the stuff," he said, "he'll come out all right. And he should have some good stuff in him. He's your son."

Pop felt beaten, but he answered: "Maybe he hasn't got all I'd like for him to have, but there's no sense making it easier for him to go wrong. He's right at the age where he's making up his mind about a lot of things."

Mike said wisely: "A man is pretty much what he is, Pop. There isn't a whole hell of a lot you can do about it."

Pop knew that, too. He was afraid the boy would come out of that winter trying to imitate Black Bill Sullivan, and Pop didn't see how he could stand it. But Mike was right. There was nothing he could do. Mike allowed very little drinking in the woods, so even that escape was out. When Pop got to thinking too much about his son's living in Black Bill's camp and learning to copy Black Bill's ways, Pop would tie into his work.

They were up before daylight every morning. They ate five times a day and sometimes didn't quit until nine o'clock at night. They felled the cloud-crashing firs and the great redwoods; they bucked them into lengths for driving; they skidded them to the river and piled them along the bank.

All day long there would be the clear ringing sound of the broadaxes, the singing cries of—"Tim-ber-r-r!"—the screech of sixteen-foot butts hitting the gravel on a greased skidway. There was the green forest, the white snow, the blue sky. There was the smell of coffee and bacon and fried potatoes in the morning, the pungent aroma of bruised pine when they sat down at noon to eat their beef-slab sandwiches, the stench of drying socks strung across the bunkhouse at night. A roaring wood fire would be in the iron stove—for the winter of 1891 in that part of Oregon was not an easy one—and tales from the deacon seat that nobody believed but everybody enjoyed.

But all these, Pop Gregory found out as the winter went far below zero, didn't help. Somehow the knowledge that his boy was out there somewhere and maybe turning out wrong was too much for him.

Mike noticed it, and one day he said: "You better get a job in town for next winter, Pop. This logging is a hard life, and you aren't a young man any more."

He said it kindly, but Pop shook his head. He kept his thoughts to himself, but they boiled inside him and made him miserable. Somehow the boy's mother had always been home in Montana, and she had been like a key log, holding everything together. But now she was gone and everything was running wild, and Pop was helpless to stop it.

In March, when it began to warm up, he didn't feel any better. In June, when the snow began to melt, Mike stretched his big arms, looked at the sun, and said: "This day is worth waiting a whole year for, Pop. This is the day when you can whip the world."

Pop Gregory stared at the mountains, silent.

Mike lowered his arms. He looked at Pop and said quietly, soberly: "Pretty soon you'll see the boy, Pop. We'll be driving in a few days."

Pop lifted his face. He looked at Mike's clear blue

eyes, and he knew from the softness in them that Mike could see the agony in his heart. He looked back into Mike's eyes and said in a low voice: "I don't want to see him, Mike. I heard from him. He's been fighting. He's licked everybody in Black Bill's crew that would take him on this winter."

Mike looked sharply at Pop. "He hasn't licked Bill, has he?"

Pop shook his head. "He hasn't fought Bill . . . yet."

Mike nodded. "He will," he said. "That's Bill's method . . . build 'em up, cut 'em down. And Bill fights like a lobo wolf. He aims to kill or cripple . . . and he knows all the tricks." Mike's blue eyes became steely. "Bill is no man for a young fellow to fight until he learns how to protect himself."

Pop wagged his head like an old man. He felt old far beyond his time. "I could stand to see him hurt better than to be a bully like Bill." He worked his jaws on nothing.

Mike said: "Maybe there's hope yet." He added cheerfully: "I have a feeling I'll whip Bill this summer. Do you suppose . . . ?"

Pop shook his head. "I don't much think so. The boy doesn't respect me. I was a pretty good fighter in my time. I can still fight, and I ain't afraid of nobody . . . but I can't lick anybody."

Mike slapped him on the back. "Whyn't you take it easy next winter and get rested up? I can get you a job in town."

Pop bristled. "The only way you can get rid of me, Mike Brady, is to fire me."

"You want to make the drive next week?"

"Sure," said Pop. "I'll go with the jam crew, same as always."

Three days later they got orders from the superintendent to drive their logs. Bill Sullivan's logs were already in the water and should be past the junction of Rock River and Crooked River by the time Mike's logs hit that point. The dam above Mike's camp was opened, and the river filled from bank to bank with icy water. They broke the rollway and poured logs into the river. Mike was foreman of the drive, but when the driving crew got strung out, he stayed close to the jam crew. The cleaning crew had done a good job on the brush and rocks in the river, and for three days the jam crew didn't wet a peavey.

Then one morning Fred Canary came riding a lathered horse alongside the river. He looked worried. "Bill Sullivan has got a jam about three miles below the mouth of Crooked River," he said. "He's been there two days now, and the logs are piling up pretty bad. I've had the dams shut off, but it's too late to do much good. A big share of the water is already in the streams, and, if we don't get these logs down pretty quick, they'll be left high and dry. Mighty big timber this year. So I want you to go down there and see if you can give Bill a lift."

Pop stared at the superintendent. Mike's lips parted, and he looked away. Then he looked back and said: "All right, I'll take my crew."

He whistled long and low, when he saw the river filled with logs. Bill had cut some really big stuff. The river for almost a mile was filled with twelve-

and fourteen-foot logs, and the pressure of millions of tons of water and thousands of logs had driven together a solid mass at the bottom end of the jam, with big logs thrown crosswise upon each other like sticks.

Bill Sullivan, his black beard heavy, was standing up on the bank shouting instructions at half a dozen men down under the breast of the jam, hunting for the key log—the one that, pried out, would cause the jam to disintegrate.

Mike went up to him and said: "Fred thought we could give you a hand."

Bill looked at him. His chest swelled.

Mike said easily: "Your men are tired. Call them off and let my boys have a pass at it."

Black Bill looked as if he was about to blow up, but there wasn't much he could do. He turned his back on Mike without answering, and barked at his men.

Mike went out on the logs, followed by Pop Gregory and Frenchy Olson and Little Jack Lanowics and half a dozen more.

Pop, at Mike's heels, was covertly looking everywhere for a glimpse of his son, but he was startled when he finally stared into the boy's thickly whiskered face. The boy was taller, maybe, and certainly heavier, but his face had a gaunt look and his eyes were red. Pop started to speak, but the boy went by without a word. Pop turned for an instant. Then he blinked his eyes and followed Mike.

They wrestled the fir and the redwood. They chained some logs back and made space. Then they worked others back, riding them as they spun in the water, cross-treading them. Eventually they

got down to the key log—a tremendous butt of redwood, eighteen feet thick, caught crosswise with
one end wedged in rocks at one side of the river.
They fought the big logs back from it, easing pressure on it.

Then Mike Brady called his men. "Up on the
bank," he ordered.

They ran light-footed along the logs. They gathered on the bank to watch Mike Brady as his blue
eyes sized up the redwood. It lay across a log of
ten-foot fir that had been driven under it until it
had raised the heavy end of the redwood fifteen
feet above the surface of the river. Mike walked out
on the high end. He stood for a moment, hatless,
with his curly hair plastered against his forehead,
stagged pants dripping water, his booted legs
braced, and his peavey planted.

"It's a tough one," muttered Little Jack.

But Pop didn't take his eyes away. "Mike'll take
it out. He's got sawdust in his veins."

The redwood was fairly well balanced on the fir,
and the fir slanted down toward the downstream
side. Mike nodded to himself. Then he leaped cat-
like down to the fir. He found his spot. He sank the
pick into the redwood and drove the cant hook in
with his boot heel. He found footing on the fir. His
shoulder muscles bunched as he got his big legs in
under the lift. The great log moved. It moved a frac-
tion of an inch, slowly, and Mike bowed his back
under the peavey. The redwood moved an inch,
two inches.

Mike straightened under the peavey like taut
steel. The redwood moved a foot and hesitated.
The light end lifted a few inches and then dipped

back. Mike heaved. The big log shuddered and started to roll. The light end came up, dripping water and muddy rocks. The log began to pivot on the fir with a great grinding of heavy bark, and the light end swung around.

Mike jerked at his peavey and started to run. But the cant hook did not come loose. He stopped to smash it with his foot. He jerked it loose, and then he ran up the fir, his caulked boots throwing out gouts of bark.

He was two-thirds of the way to safety, when the redwood, sweeping fast, caught up with him. Pop groaned, but Mike threw himself at full length on the fir. The redwood dipped, and the fir trembled. The redwood bounced and scraped over Mike's back. Then the redwood left the fir, and the fir started to move.

Mike was on his feet, running. He left the fir in a flying leap as the redwood launched into the river with a tremendous splash. He came down on a second piece of fir. It moved a little as the crest of water gathered itself to drop. Mike changed logs again, running toward shore.

The jam gave way. The level of water dropped suddenly. Mike's log went down, spinning. Mike tread on it, even when it went underwater. It came back up, and, with a tremendous crashing and a thunderous booming, the entire jam surged downstream.

Mike rode the logs with flying feet. He changed logs three times and then made a desperate leap for the bank. Pop grabbed one hand and pulled him up. Mike lay there for a moment with his face in the wet grass. Then Pop heard a loud voice: "He didn't come after your job. He came to help."

Pop cringed. The voice was his son's. Pop got to his feet. His son was facing Black Bill Sullivan. Bill's eyes were like obsidian. He lashed out with one great fist and smashed it in the middle of the younger man's face. The boy went down, but he bounced up almost as soon as he landed. He went for Bill. He hit him once, and then Bill opened up and hit him three times in the face. The boy staggered. Bill's eyes were like gleaming coals. He went after the boy. The boy straightened. He stepped in fast and laid two on Bill's chin. Bill stepped away for a moment, and the boy followed.

Then Pop Gregory found his voice. "Git back!" he shouted. "Keep away from him!"

The boy was closing in, but Pop got in front of him. The boy said grimly: "Out of my way, Dad. He's got it coming!"

"You damn' fool!" said Pop. "He'll cripple you for life."

The boy didn't see him. His eyes were on Bill. Pop stepped back and turned loose a haymaker on the boy's chin, and then a second one. The boy looked astonished as he wavered.

Pop wheeled to face Black Bill. Bill was grinning a wolfish grin. Pop took two in the face that shook him down to his caulked boots. He struck back, but blindly. He took two more, and staggered. His eyes were filled with blood.

Bill stepped back for a haymaker, and Pop heard a roaring voice: "Get away from him!"

Pop's eyes cleared a little. He made out Black

Bill, still grinning, and he went for him. But a big hand was on his shoulder. It spun him around, and Mike Brady stepped in his place.

But Pop was mad. He shoved Mike and started for Bill again. Then Mike cracked two big fists on Pop's jaw, and Pop's head went around like a log jam. His legs got wobbly, and he began to sink.

"You're an old man," Mike said softly. But the voice he used was kind. Mike said to Bill: "You want to fight?"

Bill grinned like a fiend. "My meat," he said through his black beard, and started pulling off his heavy shirt.

Mike was ready. His broad shoulders rippled smoothly. His stagged pants were pulled in tight around his waist. He looked at the mat of hair on Bill's chest, at Bill's stomach, and said: "You're getting heavy in the middle, Bill."

They were surrounded now by a ring of silent, watchful men. Bill glared from his obsidian eyes, and crouched. He rushed, and Mike met him head-on. They came together with a thud. Mike locked his arms around the big man's head and under his shoulder. Mike twisted, and Bill went over on his back. Mike tried to fall on him, but Bill wasn't there. Bill was at his back, booting him, trying to kick him in the kidneys.

Bill crouched. Blood ran from his mouth, and his face was twisted with hate. Mike had the upper hand, and Pop saw him relax, prepared for a fight that might last hours. Mike was stronger. They only thing was—could he match Bill's trickery?

Bill stepped back, breathing harshly through cut

lips. Mike slammed him on the side of the head. Bill dropped and rammed himself at Mike's legs. Then he raised and threw Mike over his back.

Mike fell on his head. Bill whirled and jumped on him. Mike raised his head, and Bill's teeth tore a piece out of one ear. Blood poured down Mike's neck. He tried to raise but couldn't. Bill was slugging him unconscious.

But Mike drew his legs up and threw them, with a twisting of his body like the snapper on the end of a whip. Bill wasn't looking for it. He went down on his face. Mike rolled and was on top of him, pounding him on the ears, driving his face into the sand. Bill heaved, and Mike rode with him. Bill was on his knees. He got up. Mike stepped in and landed hard, shattering blows that spattered blood when they landed.

Bill Sullivan wavered. Through his glazed eyes even his hate was fading. He rocked back and tried to stay on his feet, but he had met a stronger man. He started down, and Mike caught him with one last pile-driving right that snapped his head back and made his eyes roll. Bill collapsed.

Mike looked at him contemptuously, but he didn't kick him. He turned, and through his battered face he grinned. "Where's my shirt?" he asked.

Pop's boy stepped out with Mike's woolen shirt. He handed it to Mike, almost fearfully.

Mike glanced at him and took the shirt. He started to put it on and said casually: "How do you like the logging business by now?"

The boy said: "I like it." He swallowed and then

said hesitantly: "Is there any chance I could get on your crew next winter?"

Mike looked up quickly, then dropped his eyes, and began to button his shirt. "What's your name . . . your first name?"

The boy licked his lips with the tip of his tongue. "Sonny," he said at last. "Sonny Gregory."

Pop took a deep, thankful breath.

Mike said: "You can be on one of my crews next year, if you show up."

Pop looked at Black Bill, getting up, and back at Mike Brady. "What goes on here?" he asked.

"I'm superintendent next year," Mike said simply. "My crew cut the most logs this winter."

Pop smiled broadly. Then he saw his son coming toward him with his hand stretched out. "Pop, you were wonderful," he said in a low voice. "I didn't think you had it in you."

Pop blinked. "I didn't lick anybody," he blurted.

But his boy had his big young hands on Pop's shoulders. "That doesn't make any difference. You didn't hesitate to jump in and fight . . . that's what counts. When you socked Black Bill in the face, somehow it made me ashamed of the way I've been thinking about you, Pop. Seeing you step up and take your swing made all those stories suddenly come true that you used to tell me." He looked contrite. "I guess I just didn't believe you, Pop, when I came up here and saw how tough they were, and I wanted you to give me something that would *let* me believe it. Don't you see, Pop? Everything's different now. He even socked you back!"

Pop looked at his son's glowing eyes and turned away suddenly. If he was going to have tears in his wrinkled old eyes, he'd be damned the rest of his life if he wanted these hard-shelled old loggers to see it.

# Maverick Factory

Hodge Snyder cantered forward on his big, blaze-faced bay. His foreman, Rush Manso, saw him coming, and pulled his rangy grullo around to wait for him. The horse cropped at the buffalo grass while Rush leaned back against the cantle, studying Hodge with gray eyes. "Whyn't you come up the other side of the herd," Rush asked, "and stay out of the dirt?"

Hodge looked back at the trail herd—three thousand steers, some cows, and a few bulls—that wound like a long snake's trail back into the middle of the heavy dust cloud. Hodge shook his head wearily. "Take a chance on spooking a mixed herd? Not me. We had enough trouble getting 'em strung out after Vogel's outfit choused 'em up last night." He yawned. "Three nights in a row without sleep . . . and mostly on account of Vogel." He shook his head hard and forced his red-rimmed eyes open. "Anyway, the boys on the drag have been eating dirt all morning. Who am I to be fussy?"

Rush was a tall, skinny fellow who seemed all bones and angles. He crossed his arms on the flat saddle horn, and his long bones seemed to run together and relax. "Well, it's good dirt . . . the best in southeastern Colorado."

"There'll be more before we get to Cheyenne," said Hodge. He looked worried. Hodge always looked a little worried. He was a big man with light brown hair and an odd scar like a worry crease that ran straight across the bridge of his nose.

"How're they coming back there?" asked Rush, pulling the grullo's head up out of the grass.

"Not so good," said Hodge. "When we got straightened out this morning, we found four cows with burned feet."

"Burned?"

"Seared with a running iron," Hodge said shortly.

Rush tried to whistle through his dust-covered lips. "Then Vogel *was* running a maverick factory back along the Apishapa."

"He was," Hodge said positively. "Every one of them cows had a heavy bag, but no calf. Vogel took the calves and burned the cow's feet so they couldn't follow."

"What are you doing with 'em now?"

"We wrapped their feet in rawhide, and we're doing the best we can."

The front end of the herd was spreading out. Rush pushed the grullo in a little closer to keep them together and moving forward.

"It's going to be a long day," said Hodge. "I should have watched my own beef instead of chasing cow thieves with the vigilantes."

"It was the right move," said Rush. "Vogel's gang has got to be broken up before we can stop cattle stealing in this country."

Hodge was riding alongside. He scraped his dry lips with the back of a hairy hand. "Wish we could get Vogel himself."

Rush caught the eye of the man riding the left point. He threw his arm in a circle and pumped his fist a couple of times toward the north. The point rider moved in toward the herd a little.

Rush said, over his shoulder: "You'll get another crack at Vogel. There'll be grass along the Apishapa next spring, and you'll be bringing another bunch of cows up from the Concho."

"Maybe." Hodge hazed back a big, one-horned steer that came trotting forward out of the dust, head high. "Only one thing," he said. "I wish they hadn't hung them two men of Vogel's to that light pole in Pueblo."

Rush turned halfway around in the saddle. "I thought it was providential," he said. "There ain't no piñon in the country tall enough to hang a man from."

The scar on Hodge's nose became a definite worry line. "Thelma is coming in to Pueblo in the morning, and that pair of buzzard bait is the first thing she'll see." He took a deep breath. "She might get an idea the West is uncivilized."

"Proves what I said all along," said Rush. "You should have sold out, taken your traps back to Kansas City, and gone into business with Thelma's old man."

"Who . . . me?" Hodge asked indignantly.

"But," Rush went on, "as long as you didn't do that, and as long as you went and fixed it up for her to come out here with you, mebbe you better have some faith in her. Women ain't like cows, you know. They got sense. . . . Hi, you! Get back in line, there, you one-horned, mouse-colored maverick!" He yelled back at Hodge as he pushed the steer into line. "That's the critter that led the stampede last night."

Hodge nodded absently.

What *would* Thelma, with her fine manners and her fancy clothes, think of this country? To Hodge and to Rush and to ten thousand others, it was God's real country—but would Thelma see it that way?

Hodge rode out ahead to check the trail. He should have told Thelma more about what it was really like in Colorado Territory. He should have told her about the drought and parched grass along the Apishapa, the long, dusty trail days ahead on the way to new grass, the maverick factory, and men like Vogel. But he hadn't. Like a moon-eyed calf, he hadn't been able to think about anything but Thelma since the day he'd gone in to Kansas City with his last trainload of beef. He had seen her there at the stockyards with her father, sitting sidesaddle, just outside the dust around the cow pens, looking as fresh and untouched as a sunflower loaded with dew on a summer morning.

Somehow he had supposed she was used to being around cows and the dirt they kicked up and the smell they made, their incessant lowing and bawling and blatting. But now it seemed plain that he had assumed too much. Thelma had never been closer to the cattle country than the unloading pens. But by the time he'd found that out, he'd been like a dry steer headed for water—all he worried about was getting her to say yes. But now, in front of the herd and out of the dust, he saw things a little more clearly. Maybe the dust fogged a man's mind as well as his eyes. He remembered, now, little things Thelma had done and said. Any fool who could swing a barn-size loop would have known she was persnickety as an Eastern buggy horse.

A man who's spent his life in the cow country should have known that—but in Kansas City he was like an old mossyhorn that'd been dug out of the black chaparral for the first time. He hadn't seen an unattached white woman in four years, and there *she* was, sitting very straight and proud. Her hair was a dark red in the sun, and on top of it was perched a small white hat with two deep blue ribbons hanging down her back. The ribbons were the color of her eyes, which were blue and shining and laughing as she talked to her father and the brand inspectors and commission men gathered around her.

Then she had seen Hodge staring openly at her. She had looked over the size of him, and gradually worked her way to his eyes, and then for an instant her eyes were still shining but not laughing, as if she had just caught her breath. She didn't smile at him as she had been smiling at the others, but turned away hurriedly. She had smiled later, but it was a private smile and meant for nobody else but him. It wasn't a gay smile like the ones she had been throwing around the loading pens, but a quiet smile that said: "I'm yours, Hodge. I'll go with you always."

Pulling out through the deep sagebrush around a butte that stuck out like a giant bear's paw, Hodge watched the country ahead, but his mind wasn't on it. The worry crease deepened between his eyes. Thelma had been game, but he should have had sense enough to tell her what to expect. It wasn't until he was back into the cow country that he had begun to see things. Here was a girl who had lived all her life in the cities, and always had servants, and even a boy to saddle her horse. Why hadn't he told her that out in this country a woman would have to saddle her own horse? He shook his head. He was as nervous as that one-horned steer.

They crossed the Arkansas and bedded down the herd a couple of miles beyond, along in the middle of the afternoon. It was hot, and they put the herd on high ground. Hodge turned the blaze-faced bay into the remuda. He picked out a big smoky horse for himself, and a smaller calico for Thelma.

"We ain't got a sidesaddle," Rush reminded him.

"I'll buy one in Pueblo," said Hodge.

"I'm going out after a couple of stray buffalo I saw back there along the river," Rush said. He added slyly: "Reckon you'll need any help in Pueblo?"

"Where I needed help," Hodge said morosely, "was in Kansas City before I talked her into marrying me."

"It'd have been easier," said Rush, "if you had brung her on out here before you had time to think about it. But, no, you had to build a new house and all . . . and now look what happened. The house sets back there on the Apishapa, but there ain't no grass for the critters, and you're on the move, and she'll have to set up housekeeping in a covered wagon on a drive."

Hodge's jaw worked. "It's bad enough," he said, "without you driving me around the snubbing post."

Rush straightened. He seemed at last to feel pity. "Where'll we meet you?"

"I'll pick you up some time in the morning," Hodge said, and swung the smoky horse toward Pueblo. "Watch that one-horned steer," he called back. "That son will try to spook again along toward morning."

"I'll watch," said Rush. "So long."

"So long."

In Pueblo, Hodge went to the barber shop and had a bath and got shaved. Then he went out and had a drink. He said to the bartender: "Why don't they cut down those two from that light pole?"

The bartender was a short, heavy man, with skin the color of old leather and dyed black hair parted in the middle. "I hear the vigilantes wanted to leave 'em there for a warning," he said, wiping up a ring of whiskey on the bar.

Hodge looked at the bartender without seeing him. "Vogel doesn't know how to take a hint," he said heavily. He emptied the small glass and cracked it down on the bar. "Better make it two," he said. "There's a lot of dust between here and Cheyenne."

He threw out a goose, then half turned, and watched the bodies swaying from the pole. He said uneasily: "It wouldn't be quite so noticeable if the wind wasn't blowing so hard." He killed his drink and looked again from under his big eyebrows. He felt ashamed to be looking. "The one on this side keeps twisting and untwisting," he said.

The bartender sprayed change from the gold eagle in a semicircle on the bar. "Good thing the wind does blow," he said. "It keeps the buzzards from settling down."

"It's right where the stage comes in," Hodge muttered.

"No use working yourself into a state over a couple of cow thieves," the bartender said.

Hodge bought a sidesaddle for the paint, and left both horses at the livery stable. He used a broom on his boots. They were pretty wrinkled around the ankles and beginning to wear through, but they were comfortable, and he'd thought he'd wait until he got the herd to Wyoming before he spread himself.

He bought a red wool shirt, and, when he got that on and installed a beaded white buckskin vest he'd bought from an Oglala up in Nebraska a couple of years before, he began to feel pretty dressed up. The big brim of his old hat was getting a little floppy, but it would still keep the rain from running down onto his clothes. He filled the pockets of his vest with sack tobacco and papers and matches, keeping one eye on the time. Then he went to the Drovers Hotel to wait for the stage.

It was mid-afternoon when the Concord rumbled in from the east. The driver, a man with a huge mustache and an embroidered silk waistcoat and a red taffeta muffler, pulled the six horses to a stop. The brakeman took over the reins and wrapped them around the post, while the driver stepped down grandly, and headed for the saloon.

The side door of the coach opened, and Thelma appeared. The afternoon sun made her hair richly red, as he had remembered it, but this time she was wearing a light blue hat with white ribbons. She gathered her gray taffeta skirts under her and stepped down into Hodge's arms. He held her for a moment, and neither of them could say anything.

"Your baggage, Missus Snyder." The brakeman handed down a bonnet trunk. Then he saw Hodge, holding her. "You're Hodge Snyder, ain't you? Gimme a hand with this zinc-top?"

They carried her luggage to the hotel porch. "We might have to leave some of your stuff here for a little while," Hodge said uneasily.

Her slim, cool hand was inside his arm. She looked up at him. "Is something wrong, Hodge?"

"Grass dried up in the valley," he said shortly, "and we had to move the herd north. You could have stayed on the ranch, but it would be kind of lonely, and there's still a few wild Indians now and then. . . ."

"Of course, I'll go with you," she said. "When do we start?"

"We've already started. When the grass begins to dry up, you can't wait." He pointed. "The herd is over there, just south of the road you come in on. We'll catch up to them in the morning." He steered her into the hotel. "We'll have supper here, and you can get freshened up a little when we go to our room."

He felt the reassuring pressure of her slim, strong fingers. "Don't be scared," she said, "we've been married months, you know."

Hodge said: "Me scared?"

They were in the room then.

He said: "I'll open the window. It'll be warm in here."

She had taken off her hat and put the hatpins through it. Now her blue eyes shone as she said: "I'll help you."

The window came up suddenly, and Thelma shrieked. "What's that?" she cried.

Hodge swore at himself. The two cattle thieves swung from the crossarm of the light pole, right across the street from their room, silhouetted by the setting sun. The right one was turning and twisting.

Hodge stammered: "I . . ."

"Are those *men*?"

"They stole cattle," Hodge said defensively.

"Your cattle?"

He looked away, pulling in his lips between his teeth.

"Then you helped hang them?" she insisted.

"I . . . well . . . it was the vigilantes."

She looked again at the swinging figures and shuddered. "Isn't that murder?" she asked finally.

Hodge was miserable. "Some might think so . . . if they didn't know how it is out here."

"You never told me it was like this," she said accusingly.

He couldn't answer. This was what he had been afraid of.

She sat down on the bed. Her ivory face was pale. She didn't look at Hodge.

Finally he picked up his hat. "I've got to see about some supplies," he said clumsily, and lumbered out.

He went down the street to the bar and had two quick ones. The bartender looked at him curiously. "Your wife come in this afternoon?"

Hodge nodded, staring into his glass.

The bartender was twisting a corkscrew into a fresh bottle. "She going with you in the morning?"

"Yes, I reckon."

"I hear," the bartender said after a pause, "that Vogel is some put out because you short-handed him."

Hodge glanced at the man, then studied his glass. He looked around him. The saloon was filling up. Hodge shifted his six-shooter belt a little. "You hear any talk about him heading off my drive?"

"Can't say that I have, but, if Vogel was mad at me, I'd be ready for anything."

Hodge stared at him. He bought a bottle of whiskey and took it with him to the hotel. He sat down in a corner of the lobby and swung out the cylinder on his pistol. There were five cartridges in it, and one empty chamber for the hammer. He swung the cylinder back into place and shoved the pistol into its holster.

Then he started in on the bottle. He thought of Thelma's fine clothes and the lovely picture she made, and with every drink he felt more and more that he had played the fool by bringing her out to Colorado without telling her what it would be like. His guilt settled on him, and he didn't have the nerve to face her.

They rode out the next morning. Vogel's men were still swinging from the pole, but Thelma said nothing. Hodge looked straight ahead.

Thelma rode the sidesaddle easily, and they caught up with the herd about the middle of the morning. At first it was a long, rolling dust cloud, then presently they passed the cook's wagon, which was eating dirt as usual. Hodge led Thelma around the west side and out of the dust. He caught up with the drags. "How's the sore-footed cows coming?" he asked.

"We got two in the wagon there . . . the wagon you brought for you and the missus. The third one is getting along pretty good. The other one we shot."

Thelma spoke up. "What's the matter with their feet?"

"Those men you saw . . . or some of their bunch . . . used a hot iron on the cow's feet to keep them from following their calves," Hodge said gruffly.

Thelma swallowed hard.

"And that ain't all," said a hard voice behind them.

Hodge turned. Rush was riding up, with a small calf over the grullo's withers. Rush had fire in his eyes. He took hold of the calf's nose and its lower jaw and pulled its mouth open. "See that?"

Hodge glanced. He knew what to expect. But

Thelma moved closer. "What happened to it?" she asked.

"This one here," Rush said, "got its tongue split with a bowie knife."

Thelma gasped. Rush rode up to the wagon where Thelma was supposed to start housekeeping, and lowered the calf inside the tailboard with the two sick cows.

Thelma pulled up beside Hodge. "I don't understand," she said.

Hodge pulled his floppy hat brim down harder. "It's like this," he said. "A calf is always branded with the brand of its mother . . . but only at roundup time, in the spring or in the fall. In the meantime, any calf that gets separated permanently from its mother becomes a maverick . . . an unbranded critter, and anybody who tosses a rope around its neck can throw his own brand on it. Generally a calf will run with its mother till roundup time, but if men like Vogel get into a herd and cut the calves' tongues so they can't suck, and burn the mothers' feet so they can't follow the calves, pretty soon you've got a bunch of mavericks. That's why we call it a maverick factory. Vogel and his men keep an eye on the calves, and, as soon as the calves leave their mothers for good, they cut them out of the herd and brand them."

"And that's legal?" Thelma asked.

Hodge pulled his hat brim still lower. "Not exactly legal, but it doesn't leave any evidence. When there's no mother to claim her own calf, anybody who finds that calf has a right to brand it."

"In other words," said Thelma, "you've always

depended on the presence of the mother as proof of ownership."

"That's it," he said.

They rode on to the point. This was Rush's day on the windward side, but he didn't relieve the point man right away. He pulled alongside Hodge and said in a low voice: "You see that party up ahead?"

Hodge nodded, his heavy hat brim flopping.

"They're aiming to cut our trail," said Rush.

Hodge took a slow breath. "You think so?"

"They been up there by that clump of piñons for the last half hour. Now they're riding out to meet us."

Hodge shifted his gun belt.

"You better check that thing," Rush said under his breath. "You used it the other night."

Hodge looked at Thelma. She was studying the riders far ahead. Hodge said quietly to Rush: "I checked it last night. You stay with the point . . . and keep the herd moving." He rode the big smoky horse out ahead. Thelma pulled up alongside him, and he glanced at her. "You better stay back with Rush," he said.

"If there's going to be trouble, "she said, "I want to be with you."

He looked closer at her then, and for the first time he saw her red eyes. He felt bewildered.

"All right," he said, "if you've got to come, you've got to come. But this may not be nice."

She did not answer, but spurred the calico pony alongside the smoky.

The riders were coming diagonally to intersect

the path of the herd. There were five of them, and one wore a white hat. That would be Vogel, Hodge knew.

Hodge picked up his pace, but Thelma held her place at his left rear. He looked back. Rush was thirty feet behind him. Hodge turned back to the front. There wasn't any use of all of them getting killed, but he might have known Rush wouldn't hang back.

The leader of the five men cut Hodge's trail. He was a gaunt man with a black hat and long, drooping mustaches. Hodge pulled up to the gaunt man's right, so his pistol hand would not be hidden. The gaunt man said in a Yankee nasal voice: "I'm Beeson. One-eyed Turtle brand. Are you Hodge Snyder?"

"I am." Hodge's quick glance found the five men, all well-heeled.

Beeson's sharp eyes looked over Hodge's shoulder. "Them your cattle?"

"They are."

Rush pulled in at Hodge's side. Three men moved up around Beeson. Vogel, a dark-skinned, slick *hombre* in his big white hat, stayed back.

"You aiming to go north?"

"Straight north to Colorado City and Cheyenne."

Beeson's eyes settled on the crease across the bridge of Hodge's nose. "I've got a lot of stuff ahead of you."

"That's all right," said Hodge. "You can look for your brand after we get through you . . . long as you don't chouse up the herd."

But the gaunt man didn't move. "They're Texas cattle, aren't they?"

Hodge nodded, watching Vogel.

The gaunt man's voice became unexpectedly loud. "Don't trail your critters through my range," he said. "I don't aim to have three or four thousand head come down with Texas fever."

Hodge leaned hard on his saddle horn with both hands. He fastened his eyes on Beeson. "There's no Texas fever in these cattle," he said. "They wintered on the Apishapa."

Beeson's eyes narrowed. "That ain't what I heard. I heard those cattle come straight from the Concho country."

"You want to see the papers?"

"I don't trust no papers," Beeson said. "I got good, graded-up American cattle on my range, and I don't aim to have it contaminated by any Texas critters."

"The papers will show. . . ."

"You could forge the papers. I meant what I said. You ain't driving them Texas cattle over my range."

Hodge began to tighten up. "How long you been here, Beeson?"

"Three months."

"You know that man behind you in the white hat?"

"He warned me about these cattle. That makes him a friend of mine."

Hodge raised up in his saddle and found Vogel's eyes. "He's a cattle thief," he said harshly.

Vogel shrugged. He was waiting, Hodge knew, for Beeson to do his killing.

Beeson's voice was high. "You got pointers back there. Start riding in a circle."

Hodge stared at him. "I told you these cattle are clean. We're comin' through, Beeson."

The gaunt man started to reach for his pistol.

"Leave it be!" Hodge ordered, and Beeson's mouth dropped open as he stared into the muzzle of Hodge's big .44. The three men around him stopped in the act of drawing.

Rush's calm voice came from Hodge's right. "Control yourselves, gents. It's mighty unhealthy, reaching for hardware sudden-like."

"Now," said Hodge, "ride out one at a time, with your hands up, and don't make any quick moves. You, Beeson . . . you better go first!"

The gaunt man's thin lips were in a tight line. He moved his horse forward without lowering his hands. Hodge reached for the man's pistol, but froze as Vogel said sharply: "Drop those irons in the dirt, you two!"

Hodge stared for an instant. Vogel had maneuvered himself into a spot where he was covering both Hodge and Rush with two pistols. Hodge hesitated, but he had no choice. From where he was, he couldn't get a decent shot at Vogel. His jaws were hard together, and his grip on the butt of the .44 began to loosen.

But a woman's voice came from his left. "Drop those pistols, Mister Vogel."

For an instant Hodge didn't comprehend. Then he saw that Thelma, almost hidden by his own body, was pointing the muzzle of a nickel-plated Derringer at Vogel.

That could end only one way. Hodge whomped

the big smoky in both ribs and charged into Vogel's face. He scattered Beeson's men, and before Vogel could get a good shot, Hodge was in the clear.

Vogel's right pistol roared, and Hodge caught a slug in the thigh. Then his .44 exploded. For an instant Vogel looked surprised. He shot again, but it went into the dirt. He tried to raise his hand. Hodge fired again. Vogel seemed to hesitate, and Hodge poured lead into him until Vogel fell stiffly sidewise out of the saddle. He hit the ground head first. His legs pulled up once, and then he rolled over, dead.

Hodge turned his horse. Rush was covering Beeson and his men. Hodge loaded his pistol while he talked to Beeson. "This here Vogel was running a maverick factory down below the Arkansas," he told Beeson. "You want me to take you back to Pueblo to prove it?"

Beeson looked at Vogel's body. Beeson's mustaches drooped lower. He looked back up as Hodge swung the cylinder into place. "I reckon I'll take your word for it," Beeson said, staring at the pistol, "if you let me see your bill of sale."

Hodge fished a wad of papers out of his pocket with his left hand. He kept the .44 in his right. He separated the papers with his thumb and two fingers, and held one out to Beeson. "Here's a bill of sale on twenty-eight hundred and six steers that came from South Texas last summer. The cows and bulls are Colorado stock. That satisfy you?"

Beeson looked at the papers. Hodge's herd was drawing close now. The air was filling with dust and the bawling of thirsty cattle. Beeson folded the papers and handed them back. "Maybe we got taken in by a slick talker."

"That's the way it looks from here," Hodge said flatly.

Beeson sounded weary. "All right."

"You satisfied?" asked Hodge.

"I'm satisfied. Go ahead." He gestured to the north with a thin hand. "But if your cattle leave any fever," he said harshly, "you can figure on seeing me again."

Hodge grinned. "We'll figure on that," he said, and chucked his pistol in the holster.

Beeson and his men rode off slowly. Beeson glanced curiously at Vogel's body, but he looked up and saw Hodge watching him, and did not stop.

The herd was pulling up on them. Hodge rode out ahead. Then he turned to Thelma, his eyes narrowed. "Where in thundering blazes did you get that shiny little piece of hardware?" he asked.

She looked up at him, smiling in amusement. "You didn't tell me about Colorado yourself," she said, "so I read about it in the Kansas Pacific guidebook. It said most people in Colorado go armed by custom, so I bought this pistol in Kansas City. It isn't very big, but the man said it would be effective at close range. Besides, Father didn't think a pistol like yours would look good on me."

Hodge stared at her. The laughter in her blue eyes was melting him like butter in the sun. He moved the smoky toward her. Then he remembered the herd behind them. It could wait. There'd be a lot of trails for him and Thelma.

Rush had pulled into place on the point and sent his relief man back to the swing. Thelma pulled closer to Hodge. "You're a strange man," she said. "Last night you were afraid of a woman who weighs less than a hundred and twenty pounds, but today you pulled a pistol on four men at once, and then you rode square into a killer."

Hodge licked the dust from his dry lips. "Well, I . . ."

Rush rode up. "You want somebody to bury him?" he asked.

Hodge nodded.

"I'm glad you shot him," Thelma said, and shuddered. "It saved hanging him."

Hodge looked at her. She was crying. He wondered if she was going to faint. He started to put his arm around her, and then he felt the wound in his thigh. His right boot was full of blood. He leaned over, and things went suddenly black. . . .

When he woke up, he was in the wagon along with the two sore-footed cows and the split-tongued calf. He raised his head. The leg of his pants had been split and his thigh bandaged. The wagon was jerking along over the buffalo grass. He realized that his head was on Thelma's lap and her cool hand was on his forehead. Rush rode up from somewhere and looked in the back end of the wagon. "Like I always said," he told Hodge, "if things get out of hand, you better count on the woman."

Hodge looked up into Thelma's face. He noted the little valleys of dust alongside her nose. "I'm counting," he said to her, "but you better let me have that little cannon before it hurts somebody."

"You are in no position to be disarming a defenseless woman," she said.

Hodge looked at her eyes; they were very tender. He took a deep breath and relaxed. "Anyway, I'm no maverick," he said. "You've got your brand on me for good."

# Grandfather Out of the Past

Tuchubarua was an old, old man. The hot sun of countless summers on the *Llano Estacado* and the driving sleet storms of the West Texas breaks had etched into his ancient, copper-colored Comanche face a pattern of wrinkles that spoke of experience, of wisdom, of love and hate, and violent passions now long subsided but not quite forgotten, of exploits on the hunt, on raids, on the warpath, of bloody scalps, of captive women, of long and weighty councils. But all those days of glory were gone, and in the wake of his hundred and twenty-six summers were only memories—some of them a little dim—and an old man making arrows for the young warriors, for his great-grandsons and his great-great-grandsons and his great-great-great grandsons. He was an old man from whom ineffable age had stripped all glory and all egotism and all vanity, leaving in their place only a desire to live—to survive in a hard land and with a savage

people where usefulness was the only excuse for
existence, where a man too old to hunt was also too
old to eat. Since Tuchubarua's strength was not
equal to the making of a saddle or a bow, and since
he had, forty years before, given away most of his
power, his only remaining usefulness was in the
arrows he made. His eyes now saw but dimly
things that were near him, and so he had only his
ancient knowledge and the skill of long experience
to stand between him and banishment to the open
prairie.

He felt a heavy step on the hardpacked ground
and knew, without looking up, who had made it,
and prepared himself as he slowly drew a slender
dogwood shaft through the arrow straightener.
The squat figure of Quahuahacante, Dead Hide,
stopped before him, and Tuchubarua looked up
slowly.

"Old Man," said Quahuahacante in his harsh
voice, "I told you to have four arrows for me today."

Tuchubarua's voice in answer was soft and liquid and flowing, like those of most Comanches,
and the only evidence of his great age was in the
occasional failure of his voice at the end of a word.
"An arrow takes time," he said. "It must wing
straight and true, and it is not easy to make them
so when the wood is not properly seasoned."

Quahuahacante snorted. "Excuses are no good,
Tsukup."

Quahuahacante, who was in his forties and as-
pired to be a war leader, always called him Old
Man. Others, too, called him Old Man, but they
used the word *narabuh*, which was a term of familiarity. Most members of the tribe, however, called

him Tuchubarua, Bear Bird, for that was the name by which he had signed the great treaty with the Kiowas in 1790. Quahuahacante alone called him Tsukup.

It made no important difference, for Tuchubarua was a very old man, and his only remaining desire was to live out his days, however many they might be, among those of his own blood. He sighted along the shaft, taking his time, hoping that Quahuahacante, in his impatience, would go away, for Tuchubarua, relying entirely on his wrinkled fingers and their still fine sense of touch, had to conceal his failing eyesight.

"Note well, Tsukup," said Quahuahacante. "We won't need arrows much longer anyway, for the white men are coming with rifles that shoot many times . . . faster even than a bow."

Tuchubarua looked up from the arrow and saw the hard malevolence in the younger man's eyes. Why was it, he wondered, that some men never were satisfied to leave things as they were? Long, long ago, before he had reached his hundredth birthday, the band had accepted Tuchubarua as a fixture, and nobody had questioned his right to a small portion of meat when there was some extra. He did not require very much, and he never took the good parts. The hump, the tongue, the brains, the liver, the kidneys, the fleeces—all those he left to others, while he was grateful for a piece of brisket or even a small length of tail, and, when food was very scarce and the babies cried, he could go without food many days.

Meanwhile, other Comanches had died off, generation by generation, and presently all of his sons and grandsons were gone. In Comancheria, without any form of written record, it was hard for any person to be conscious of anyone else more than two generations before him, so Tuchubarua found himself, without warning, a forgotten legend that had to be fed. Most of them did not seem to mind, but Quahuahacante had a reason for wanting Tuchubarua out of the way, for his power would never be complete with the old man around. Tuchubarua had seen him in a moment of weakness, and such was the Comanche psychology that, even though Tuchubarua had never told, Quahuahacante *knew* he had been seen, and the knowledge would be a gnawing thing as long as Tuchubarua lived.

All these things were in Tuchubarua's mind as he looked into the flinty black eyes of the younger man, and tried hard to recall whether he himself had ever been as heartless and as determined. It was hard to know, because one who had erred as Quahuahacante had erred must have strange and powerful desires.

Tuchubarua watched the black eyes that always showed a gleam when they looked at a girl or a woman, and he wondered at the strangeness of the young man's desires. In sexual matters there were few restraints for the Comanches, and, as a result, inhibitions were not common—certainly not in the males. It meant, however, that those taboos that did exist must be scrupulously observed, or the combined weight of the tribal disapproval would fall on the violator. A man's sexual activities were largely not subject to censorship. He might start very early trying to make babies with girls his own age, or he might be taught by older women; the only taboo was against incestuous relationships. When he became a little older, he could visit the girls in their parents' teepees, or he could receive them in his teepee, and the only rule was that the boy must not make the advance. If he did, he was in tribal disgrace. If he forgot himself so far as to stay with a girl all night, he was considered married.

As he grew older, he watched the warriors use captive women, and experimented with them himself; still later, his sex activities would involve older women of the Comanches. He was expected to use his brothers' wives, and he would find himself with the wives of other warriors, also—the only restraint in the latter case being that, if he should be caught with a married woman, he would have to pay damages for the use of another man's property.

But with all this freedom, Quahuahacante had strange and hidden desires, and Tuchubarua was well aware of them—so well aware that it was a wonder that Quahuahacante did not recognize his feelings; but the younger man was too intent on himself to pay attention to another's thoughts.

"You are an old man," Quahuahacante said, "who has lived long past his time."

Tuchubarua did not answer.

The younger man turned on his heel and strode away—a ridiculous gesture in a Comanche, for they always looked awkward on foot.

After a moment, Tuchubarua slowly drew the arrow through his fingers, thankful that he could still sense the deviations. Then with slow movements and great care he fitted the wood again into the hole in the sandstone slab, turning the arrow to scrape it at the right place.

A soft voice from behind him said: "Tawk, you are working early. The sun is not yet at its height."

He turned. Only one person called him Grandfather any more: his great-great-great-granddaughter, the image of his first wife—a slender, smiling Shoshoni woman who had been carried off one night by the Utes. To the best of his hundred-year-old memories, this girl, Ekarraw-ro, She Blushes, was descended from the Shoshonis. It was hard to be sure over such a long time and so many wives, but it made no difference to Tuchubarua. Ekarraw-ro was a good girl; she worked hard, when she had work to do; she laughed easily; and she played hard. She did not, however, visit boys' tents at night, nor did she go walking on the prairie with them in the dark. Not that chastity was precious to the Comanches—but there was an extra pride about a girl who did not give herself away. He looked at Ekarraw-ro approvingly. She was a ripe fifteen, and the laughter in her eyes meant that she had much to give.

"There are arrows to be made," he said.

She leaned over to pick up a dogwood shaft from the bundle.

He watched her slim, well-shaped figure appreciatively. If she had not been his own kin, he would have reached for her.

"Tawk," she said, gently scolding, "these shafts are too crooked for any good use. Where did you get them?"

"Quahuahacante brought them," he said, and realized for the first time that the young warrior had done it deliberately. He looked up at her, and she was sober, avoiding his eyes. Then she knew, also.

But she did not embarrass him, for that was the great damage one might do to a Comanche: catch him in an embarrassing position, either taking advantage or being taken advantage of. She said instead: "I'll gather you some straight pieces, Tawk, so it will not be such hard work."

He considered. Quahuahacante, then, knew about his eyes. At a distance he could see well, but within the length of his arms he was half blind. Quahuahacante knew that and must have been giving him crooked shafts for a long time. They were only slightly crooked, of course, but it would have been noticeable to a man with good eyesight. Tuchubarua began to feel a little discouraged then, for the first time in his long life, because it was plain that Quahuahacante was trying to force him into banishment, and for a moment Tuchubarua wished that he had had many daughters. Out of twenty-two or twenty-four children by his many wives—it was hard to remember which unless he should count them in his mind—all but two had been sons. Those two had died of the disease that pitted a man's face, and he had had no daughters to marry into other families of influence and thus perpetuate his position with the tribe. Most of his sons and grandsons had been good warriors but not war leaders or chiefs; many had died young— not uncommon among the Comanches; and without quite knowing how it had happened, he one day had found himself isolated, a lone chief at the head of an ordinary family.

Later, he had picked out a fine young warrior

and had given away all of his power except that
which protected him from harm to his good name.
He had intended to deliver that, also, but the
young man was killed on a raid into Mexico, and
Tuchubarua was left unexpectedly with only a
small power and without an important friend in
the tribe.

That had been sixty years before, and even then
Tuchubarua was too old to fast to gain more power,
and too poor to get it from a medicine man, nor
was he entirely willing to accept blindly all the restrictions that might go with it. Great power was a
fine thing, but it was for the young, because great
power carried great responsibilities and many restrictions, and it took a young man of alert mind to
live with all those restrictions and not violate
them. For, while few powers protected a man from
death, all power was dangerous; when a Comanche offended his medicine, his power would
punish him, and the usual punishment was death.

His medicine in this case was the body of a dried
baby horned toad that he wore in a buckskin locket
on his neck. It had only a small restriction attend-
ing it. He must not eat certain foods: bear, coyote,
fish, snakes. It was a very minor restriction, because those foods were taboos to Comanches anyway, and so he had not been in a hurry to give
away the power. There was also, now that he recalled, a minor secondary restriction: he could not
stand on his feet and talk in public before a group
that included any woman whom he knew to have
violated any serious taboo.

His mind was still sharp, and those things went
through it almost instantaneously, and he watched

Ekarraw-ro standing as straight as the arrows he made, and he noted her full breasts, no longer pointed like a girl's but round like a woman's, and he observed her round, solid hips under the buckskin skirt. Then he looked away quickly before she should see how closely he was observing her—and caught the black eyes of Quahuahacante, also watching her.

In spite of his age, Tuchubarua felt repelled when he looked into the evil eyes of Quahuahacante, but the younger man made no gesture or grimace to reveal his thoughts. He turned away, once again in that ridiculous stride.

Tuchubarua looked up at Ekarraw-ro and surreptitiously fingered the dried horned toad within his shirt. "Kaku, you must not go for reeds without an older woman."

She looked at him curiously. "Grandfather, do not worry. No boy would dare risk his standing in the tribe by approaching a girl . . . and I am not going to invite them."

He looked at the arrow straightener. "These are evil times," he said. "I urge you not to go out of sight of camp alone."

She nodded agreeably. "And I have a request of you, Grandfather."

He looked up. "Yes?"

"I have seen a young man watching me. He may, I think, want to marry me."

He went a little cold at those words, but showed nothing in his face. "Yes?"

"I wish you to handle the arrangements for me, Grandfather Out of the Past."

"Your father . . ."

"My father was killed by the Pawnees last fall."

He remembered.

"All my mothers are dead." She meant her mother and her mother's sisters, and he noted with approval that she refrained from mentioning the name of any dead person—for that was taboo. "Therefore," she said, "I ask you to make the arrangements." She looked at him and said softly: "I am not able to give you a present, Grandfather, but you may keep all the ponies you get for me."

"What need have I for ponies?"

"None, perhaps . . . but the price must be high."

He smiled. She had a great deal of pride. "What is the young man's name?" he asked.

"Black Antelo . . ." She blushed.

He smiled again. "He is an honest man and has been a good warrior. He will make a good husband and father."

"He may not ask," she said nervously.

"I think he will."

He knew whereof he spoke. Among the Comanches some matches—especially those between an older man and a girl—were matters of convenience, but where both were young—Black Antelope was only twenty-four—it could be assumed that love played a far bigger part than either one let on. But those were thoughts that an old man kept to himself.

She looked up at him and saw the assurance in his ancient face, and then her thoughts turned to something else. "Black Antelope's mother and father are giving a Buffalo Tongue Feast tonight, and I am to serve the tongue."

He looked at her shining eyes, and smiled. It

was an honor for her and for Black Antelope's parents, too, for there was a small chastity test connected with the serving. It made him feel warm all over, for it showed they respected her and wanted to show her off a little before the tribe. It would not be a vain sort of showing off, but a quiet exhibition of pride, and as such was not taboo.

"And you are to come, Grandfather Out of the Past, and eat tongue until you can hold no more."

His ancient face wrinkled with pleasure. The Buffalo Tongue Feast was a gay affair, as were a good many Comanche celebrations, but of late years they had tended to forget Tuchubarua. Then his face sobered as he realized that only Ekkarawro had invited him—but it was not her party. He nodded, however, and watched her gracefully walk away. It would be nice to see her serve the tongue, for while it was no disgrace for a girl to have had relations with a man, it was nice *not* to have had relations. The possibility that any man would dispute her chastity was remote, for no girl who was not a virgin would so expose herself to ridicule. It would be far less reprehensible to have lain with many men than to have claimed virginity when one did not have it.

She went away, and he resumed his work. Ten ponies would keep him the rest of his life. He wondered if Ekarraw-ro had his security in mind. Drawing the arrow slowly through the hole, he realized that he would not be able to keep the ponies. It would be too obviously a greedy thing, and even an old man like him was not oblivious to the weight of the tribal censure. Perhaps he could give them to some family that would in turn agree to provide meat for him. In such a case he would no longer be a tribal responsibility, and Quahuahacante would have no excuse for suggesting his disposal. But he knew, even as he thought it, that such a course could never be. A Comanche could not beg—and giving away to get something in return was begging.

He sat there with the warm sun on his back, drawing the shafts through the straightener, taking his time. It was a long time till evening, and he had no pot of meat to appease his hunger in the meantime unless somebody invited him. In the evening everybody in the camp was fed; that had always been the rule. But in between times, a man was on his own.

He said—"Hmp!"—aloud as he considered Quahuahacante's implied threat that arrows would lose their value. He had first heard that back in the 1730s. He had been young then, and it had impressed him; now he was old, and not many things impressed him.

Arrows had changed since those days, for in olden times they had made arrows with only two feathers, where now they used three. Those were the days of raids on the Spanish, whose women made the best wives of all. Those were the days of great raids against the Jicarillas and the Navajos and the Tejanos, the days of the *contrabandistas* from Arkansas with many goods, of long smokes around the campfire, with plenty of *pah'mo* traded (or sometimes raided) from the Spanish, of buffalo-hunting on a good horse, of captive women and many scalps. . . .

* * *

He was almost asleep when, again, he heard the soft pad of feet on the clay, and looked up to see a comely squaw, Wading in Still Water, coming toward him, and watched her appreciatively, for Comanche women, unlike the men, were very graceful on foot. He looked up, shading his eyes with his hands, tossed his two braids back over his sun-warmed shoulders, and waited for her to speak.

"Bear Bird," she said, "I am a woman, and I have not passed the menopause, and so I cannot smoke with you, but I would visit."

He made room for her to sit across the stone from him, and carefully resumed his work. "I am honored to have you here," he said, placing an arrow in the straightener.

After this palaver had gone on for a while, Wading in Still Water came to the point. "My nephew, Black Antelope, wishes to marry your granddaughter, Ekarraw-ro."

He nodded without looking up. He was pleased that Ekarraw-ro was to get her wish so soon—although that was not unusual, for marriages among the Comanches moved fast, once there was a meeting of minds. And he had not the slightest doubt that Ekarraw-ro had correctly interpreted the questing looks of Black Antelope—for in affairs of the heart among the young, looks given and accepted might well constitute a meeting of minds.

"Black Antelope is young, but he is a brave warrior," she said, "and under the teaching of Stinking Bear he has become one of the best horse thieves of the Penatekas."

He nodded. He had heard about Black Antelope's competence with horses, but he observed: "He has gambled them away."

"It is only because he had nothing else to do with them. He is a generous man and sought to keep nothing for himself."

"Perhaps that would continue to be so."

"He is a thoughtful man, also. He will take fine care of his wife and children."

The palaver went on and on, he objecting, she countering. They both knew how it would turn out, but as protector of the girl he must not seem eager; it was against Comanche custom.

Finally Wading in Still Water said: "My nephew has just come back from a raid on the soldiers at Fort Belknap. He has many horses and will give you ten of the finest for the hand of your grand-daughter."

His reply was slow. "I will have an answer for you tomorrow."

They both knew what the answer would be. The man and the girl were young; it would be a love match. Ekarraw-ro would be the *naraibo*, or first wife. What more could anyone ask?

Ten ponies were a fine price from a young man, and Black Antelope had demonstrated his generosity by offering them immediately without haggling; likewise, Tuchubarua had tacitly accepted, since he had not rejected the offer but had preserved appearances by setting a conventional period for deliberation—one of the many conventions that were extremely important to Comanches.

"Thank you, Narabuh," she said. "And now tonight my husband and I are giving a Buffalo Tongue Feast. You are to be the guest of honor."

He looked up abruptly. "I will be glad to help you celebrate, but for forty years I have had no wife to care for my clothing, and so I cannot be a guest of honor."

She joked with him. "What's the matter, Narabuh? Doesn't a woman arouse desire in a young fellow like you?"

His ancient eyes squinted, and he drew in a deep breath. "Such a woman as you can still arouse me," he said. "Now go away, because I have no money to pay damages to your husband."

She smiled kindly at him. It meant nothing personal; the Comanches were not prudish; and it was quite usual for men and women to talk frankly to each other. But his blood was racing through his ancient veins as he watched her leave, and he sighed as he went back to his arrows. An old man without money and without much power was in a bad situation.

He continued to work on the arrows, and presently Ekarraw-ro came, gay and bubbling with her knowledge, and laid down a bundle of mulberry shafts. "These are better than your dogwood, Grandfather."

She brought him a drink from a buffalo paunch, and after a while he told her that Wading in Still Water had asked him for her hand.

"How many ponies did you demand?" she said.

"Ten." He looked at her. "Do you think that is too many?"

She said with forgivable scorn: "Black Antelope

can steal more horses than any ten men in the band. We should have asked a hundred."

He shook his head. "Ten horses show pride. Twenty horses would show greed."

She nodded, her eyes on him. "You are right, Grandfather Out of the Past. Here." She gave him something warm, wrapped in a piece of rawhide. "Wading in Still Water is giving away meat to all, for Fights with a Knife killed four buffaloes with the lance, and everybody will have meat."

He nodded. "It is good not to be hungry."

She looked at him soberly. "Are you sometimes hungry, Grandfather?"

He looked at her, trying to decide what hunger was. Was it a gnawing in a man's stomach, or was it a lonesomeness of the heart, or was it, sometimes, a thing that ate a man's brain from the inside, like that which showed in the eyes of Quahuahacante, Dead Hide? "No," he said, clutching his medicine through his shirt. "No, I am not really hungry." He unrolled the rawhide and found a chunk of steaming, half-bloody meat. His mouth watered, and he said carefully: "It looks like a tender piece of shoulder."

"It is," she said. "There is plenty more if you want it."

He shook his head. No, he would fill up on tongue that night—and he had not had tongue for many years.

Ekarraw-ro stayed for a few minutes and then went to her teepee, that had been her father's. Tuchubarua sat for a long time, chewing his meat, savoring the rich, smoky flavor—for Wading in Still Water was old-fashioned; she did little of the boiling that most Comanche women had adopted when they had begun to get brass kettles from the white traders. Tuchubarua still had a number of good teeth, and he took his time, enjoying the bloody center of the meat. When he had finished, he licked his fingers and rubbed his hands in the dirt to clean them, and leaned back for a while against a mound of earth. He wished he had some tobacco to smoke, but that was truly a luxury not readily available to an old man in his position, so he put it out of his mind, and rested, and let his ancient eyes rove slowly over the village—the forty cone-shaped tents, the cottonwood trees in the stream behind them, the grass-covered hills beyond.

It was mid-afternoon, and adults were either sleeping or doing work that required little exertion. Two buffalo hides were pegged out on the grassy slope beyond the camp, but it was too hot to work in the sun. The women were sewing clothing, if they were young and ambitious, or doing nothing, if they were older. The men would be preparing their faces, painting their chests and arms, taking care of their hair in preparation for the Buffalo Tongue Feast.

Across the creek to the left of the camp, four small boys, naked and almost black from the sun, stalked hummingbirds with arrows split at the ends to capture the birds rather than kill them, so they could experiment with them. Older boys of ten to twelve lay in the shade of mesquite bushes, or worked on long pieces of orange-yellow *bois d'arc* to make their own bows, and one was down at the stream, talking to two girls getting water, and undoubtedly trying to arrange a playing-chief party. Tuchubarua chuckled. In two more years they would go to fantastic lengths to avoid any girl. The tribal taboos were rigid in many matters, and Tuchubarua recalled with stern sadness the older brother of Ekarraw-ro who shot and killed a girl who had approached him unwell. It was a harsh thing to do, but those were the tribal mores, and the boy's parents did not even have to pay damages when the girl's parents ascertained the true situation.

Tuchubarua heard an angry buzz over his head, and looked behind him to see two five-year-olds pursuing it with glee. In a moment they had captured the horsefly and pushed a stem of grass into its anus and turned it loose.

Tuchubarua fell asleep and woke up on his side, aware that somebody was standing near him. He rose to a sitting position, blinking.

"Bear Bird," said a woman's voice, "you are older than you were. I can remember when you never slept in the sun."

He got his eyes open quickly. The husky, taunting voice was that of Sits by Herself, a sister of Quahuahacante.

He said: "I do not need to apologize for my age."

"You should have apologized twenty years ago."

He studied her. Sits by Herself was the most beautiful woman of the tribe. He suspected she had Mexican blood, but it made no difference. Even now, in her late thirties, her skin was smooth, her face oval, her hair glossy. And she had not developed the extreme heaviness usual to Comanche women—perhaps because she never had married, never had borne children.

When she was seventeen, Tuchubarua wanted to marry her and had made an arrangement with her parents, but she had been unwilling. Of course, there had been a great age difference between them, but she had not seemed to object to it. She had, however, suggested that they try it first, before they started living together. That was not unusual, and he had agreed—puzzled somewhat, however, at the cold manner in which she made the proposal. They had ridden over the hill to a place he had prepared, with a buffalo robe on the warm sand and willows for privacy, and, as they approached the trysting place, he began to realize that, with all her beauty, the girl aroused nothing within him. It was a puzzle, for she was lithe, strong, solid of body. She took off her clothes, and he knew by her actions that she had been with men before, but he was repelled by the awful coldness that enveloped her. After a raid and killing and scalping, it would not have mattered to him—but this was love-making, and she did not help him. She was willing, but with about as much interest as a sandy beach in the winter time. To his final great embarrassment, he had been unable, and they had ridden back to the village in silence, and the marriage had been canceled. He never had known for sure whose fault it was, but one thing he had known: it had never happened to him before. And later he knew that she felt the guilt rather heavily, for, when they were alone, she never failed to remind him. And her talk was not the good-natured banter of other Comanches, but words with barbs.

The Comanche way would have been to tease him in public. But she did not.

He looked at her again. She still had beauty outside, but she had coldness—even hostility—inside the lovely body. Tuchubarua well knew that a number of other men besides himself had tried to get her, but she had not married, and he wondered if she had treated each one the way she had him. Perhaps she was aware of her lack, and had enough decency to reveal it before she married—but afterward said sarcastic things to her victims to bolster her own pride.

All those things went through Tuchubarua's mind, and he wondered how many other men in the band were subject to her periodic sarcasm. One might have suspected that she was not properly formed, but few malformed Comanche babies lived very long; besides, he had seen the necessary evidence with his own eyes. He looked now into her face, and waited for her to go on.

She wasted little time. "My brother, Quahuahacante, asks for the hand of She Blushes . . . Ekarraw-ro."

He studied her. "Quahuahacante has four wives," he said.

"He is an important man in the band," she told him. "He has many and great powers, and he needs another wife to take care of his shield."

There had to be an excuse, of course. A man with four wives might be thought uxorious, if he should take a fifth, but if he had a practical need, it was different.

He wanted time. "What does he offer?"

"He offers the pick of any pony except his gray war pony and the bay buffalo hunter."

She certainly was a different woman from Wading in Still Water. After Wading in Still Water had spoken half a dozen words, a man began to think of the bed, even though he had no design on her. But after half a dozen words with Sits by Herself, a man thought of ponies or arrows. Tuchubarua, for all his hundred and twenty-six years, felt a quickening of his blood when he was around Wading in Still Water, but around Sits by Herself he felt nothing, as he had before.

Tuchubarua said, choosing his words carefully: "It is a great honor to receive an offer from Quahuahacante, but Ekarraw-ro has been already promised."

For a moment she stared at him incredulously. "I have heard nothing of this," she said. "Why hasn't she married, then?"

He squinted into the sun. "The offer was made only a little while ago." He was conscious that he was telling a small lie, but he thought perhaps he might be forgiven for it.

"I don't believe it!" Sits by Herself said.

"It is true."

She stared at him for a moment with that strange coldness—sometimes he thought it was hatred—and then turned and left, walking rapidly, not with the grace of Ekarraw-ro or Wading in Still Water. He watched her until she disappeared among the teepees. Sometimes it seemed to him that his long life had been wasted, for there were still many questions about men and women that he could not answer.

Comanche life tended to be fairly simple; when it departed from that pattern, even the wisest old men found it hard to understand.

Among the teepees had appeared the next oldest man of the band—Hichapat, the Crafty One. Hichapat was only sixty-five or so, but he was considerably bent over and walked with a cane. He had been a great warrior when men like Pedro Vial and José Charvet had been interpreters for the Spanish at Santa Fé—and that was a long time ago. Tuchubarua watched him, wondering if the old man was coming up for a chat. Perhaps he would bring a pipe and tobacco—although Tuchubarua well knew that Hichapat had no more chance at tobacco than he himself.

Hichapat had one advantage, however: he was a grandfather of one of Quahuahacante's wives, and so he would never be left on the prairie to die.

"Tawk!"

He turned. Ekarraw-ro was behind him. Her black eyes turned from the place where Sits by Herself had disappeared. She looked at him, and her liquid eyes softened. "Tawk, I have another present for you." She gave him a rawhide bag.

He smelled it without raising it, and stared at her. *"Pah'mo!"* The copper-black skin around his ancient eyes crinkled with delight. "Tobacco!"

She touched the back of his hand. "They offered me a present for serving at the feast."

He took a deep breath, the better to admire the aroma. He looked up at her. "You should have gotten something pretty," he said.

She shrugged and tossed her hair. "To please you is the greatest need I have until I get a husband."

For a moment his heart was so full that his eyes felt watery. Then he said: "You have given me a memorable day, Kaku."

Her eyes danced. "I may need your help later . . . making arrows for my husband."

He laid the bag on a rock at his side. There was no hurry. For a while he would savor the aroma. "Would you like to marry Quahuahacante?" he asked, watching her.

For a moment she stared at him. Then she turned ashen. "Quahuahacante?" she whispered.

He waited.

Finally she recovered and asked: "How many horses does he offer?"

"One.

"It is not enough," she said.

He nodded slowly and for a long time. "I told her you were already promised."

Her eyes were inscrutable. "It is a good answer, Grandfather Out of the Past. I would run away before I would marry that one."

He wondered how much she knew. "You do not like him?"

She looked at him, her thoughts far away. He could not tell whether she knew or not, but he doubted it. "He is unclean," she said finally. "It is in his eyes."

"Unclean" meant a great many things in Comancheria: probably some violation of taboos or of restrictions on a man's power. Tuchubarua considered her words for a moment and then decided that the answer was in what she had said: she had seen it in his eyes. Tuchubarua was satisfied; he knew there were some things about a man that a woman could sense, whether or not she had any knowledge of the facts.

"I will give the answer to Wading in Still Water when she comes tomorrow," he said.

She smiled. Her clouded eyes turned into dancing lights. "I will go now, to get ready for the feast," she said, and turned with a swirl of her buckskin skirt.

Hichapat, the Crafty One, was approaching slowly. Tuchubarua sat back and waited for him. Hichapat came up, nodded, and sat cross-legged on the ground. His bad leg, that had been gored by a buffalo bull in his youth, gave him some trouble, and it took time for him to arrange it comfortably.

"It is a good day," he said at last.

Tuchubarua nodded. "The grass is growing tall and green, and the ponies will be fat by the time the buffalo arrive," he said.

Hichapat considered that for a while. "If it grows too fast," he observed, "it will be full of water, and that is not good."

This was the idle chitchat of old men. It went on for a while, with Tuchubarua enjoying the aroma of the tobacco still in the pouch. Across the camp, Wading in Still Water was directing the second and third wives in preparation of the meat. They were wrapping the big tongues in grass and leaves and clay and burying them in hot coals. He moistened his ancient lips as he anticipated the savory meat, and he drew a deep breath as he considered the prospect of getting his belly full for the first time in months.

He decided to go to his teepee. He took his time but arose rather easily for a man of his age. Hichapat, of course, did not move or even look up. Tuchubarua went to the old *awyawt* at the back of his teepee. The rawhide bag, a companion on many trails, had been made for him by a young Ute squaw whom he had captured on a raid. She had been a good wife and easy to get along with, complaining only when he neglected to call her to his bed; he remembered her fondly. She had been adept with rawhide and had made for him many containers: a tobacco pouch, a bag for his mirror and tweezers, a cover for his shield, and the *awyawt*, and in it he kept his few remaining possessions against the day when he might be left alone on the sun-baked prairie.

Secretly, from time to time, he had salvaged a few items that might be useful to him in such an extremity—a bone needle and some dried deer sinew; the uppers of a pair of moccasins discarded by a wife of Quahuahacante. And his pipe, almost as old as he was. The bone stem had long been broken, and he had carved a new mouthpiece at the broken end; the bowl was blackened and chipped; the paintings had worn off; the sinews on which beads had once been strung had long been broken, and the beads had been lost; and without a wife, he could not redecorate it, for that was not a warrior's work. But then—he sighed as he drew it from its resting place and slowly unwrapped the rawhide covering—he was no warrior any more, and he told no more stories around the campfire, for none would listen; he boasted no longer of the horses he had stolen from the Mexicans, the women he had brought home to his teepee, or the Ute and Apache scalps that had once decorated his scalp pole. The pipe now was for him only a source of pleasure in itself.

Bearing the pipe in both hands, he went back to the rock and sat down. Hichapat looked up once, saw the pipe, and looked back at nothing. It would have been impolite to show undue curiosity.

Tuchubarua took tobacco leaves from his pouch, rolled them in his palms, crushed them carefully, wishing he could save all of the fragrance. Hichapat looked up and began to watch, no emotion showing on his face. Tuchubarua filled the pipe, packed it down, and started to get up to go for a light. But Ekarraw-ro appeared with a burning twig, and handed it to him. He glanced at her silently, for this was a ritual not to be interrupted by words. She smiled and went away. He puffed on it four times and then gravely handed it to Hichapat, who puffed four times and handed it back.

"Your granddaughter," said Hichapat, "will make a good wife."

Tuchubarua nodded slowly, his eyes half closed. "She is a hard worker," he observed.

"Quahuahacante has been watching her," Hichapat observed.

"I know." He handed the pipe to Hichapat.

"You would like such a match?" Hichapat asked curiously.

Tuchubarua considered his answer. "He already has many wives," he said.

Hichapat drew four times on the pipe. "He is a strange man. His mother was a Jicarilla, and his grandfather was a mountain man."

Tuchubarua took the pipe but did not answer.

"If he is rejected," Hichapat went on, "he will be a mortal enemy."

"Why should he want Ekarraw-ro?" asked Tuchubarua. "He has many wives . . . all from prominent families. There is Whistling, who makes his teepees . . . there is Burning Grass, who takes care of his shield and his war equipment . . . there is Mane of a Horse, who is a good cook and can make food out of nothing . . . there is Dry Wood, who . . ." He paused, for Dry Wood was Hichapat's granddaughter.

Hichapat observed him levelly through eyes of age and wisdom. "Who goes walking naked in the night with any young warrior," he finished.

Tuchubarua moistened his lips but said nothing.

"Why does she not stay in his teepee at night?" Hichapat asked rhetorically. "She was a good girl. She was not too free with the boys before she married. She wanted to be a wife. Why is she not satisfied?"

Tuchubarua puffed at the pipe. "It is perhaps even stranger," he said, turning the conversation, "that Quahuahacante does not bring a claim for damages against the guilty warriors."

Hichapat took the pipe. "It is his swollen vanity," he said.

Tuchubarua was silent, for vanity of that nature was not Comanche-like.

"And perhaps," Hichapat added, staring at the pipe, "he is afraid of what might come to light."

Tuchubarua was silent again. Yes, fear. It was something a Comanche might feel, but not something that he might ever reveal. On the other hand, what kind of warrior was Quahuahacante to allow one of his wives to submit herself to other braves and do nothing about it? That was one of the greatest Comanche sins of all: failure to insist on his rights.

Presently the pipe was smoked out. Hichapat scraped the bowl with a twig. Then he got up painfully with the help of his cane. "There will be plenty of tongue tonight," he said.

Tuchubarua watched him hobble away. What *would* be Quahuahacante's motive for wanting Ekarraw-ro?—to show his power, or perhaps to prove something to himself, to give himself confidence? Perhaps. But Tuchubarua was determined on one thing: Ekarraw-ro would never be submitted to Quahuahacante's dark designs, whatever they were. Anyway, it was too late now. She was promised—at least in his mind.

He wrapped up the pipe and put it away, with the tobacco pouch beside it. Then he made himself comfortable on his worn, old buffalo robe and got ready to take his afternoon nap. He had not made much progress on the arrows that day, but he would work hard tomorrow.

From across the camp he could hear the women chattering like magpies, children running and shouting. He knew that somewhere Ekarraw-ro was rubbing her best dress with white clay to make it spotless, and perhaps looking for extra beads or porcupine quills to decorate it. Old Tuchubarua had a very warm feeling when he contemplated the fullness of her heart as she made herself ready for the feast.

\* \* \*

It was black down below the Caprock when he awoke. The heat of the day was gone, and in its place was the cool night wind from the west, blowing across the endless prairie and under the purple-black sky with its brilliant stars, to drop into the little valley of the Quinatafue and carry away the heat of the scorching sun.

Before the teepee of Wading in Still Water and her husband, three fires in a row burned brightly—a prodigal waste of wood in a country where wood was scarce—but a Buffalo Tongue Feast was not held every night. And now the flickering flames from the cedar boughs played against the mystically painted teepees, where women and children and a few warriors were already gathering.

The savory odor of roast tongue came to Tuchubarua's old nostrils, and he hurried to make his meager toilet. He rebraided his gray hair, with the larger braid on the left; he scoured the bottom of a horn container for a precious smudge of vermilion for his cheeks; he took off his frayed breechclout, shook it out, and put it back on. He had no leggings and only the one pair of moccasins; those were soiled, but they would have to do. Anyway, what business had an old man with vanity? He put on his buckskin jacket; once it had been white and gay with red and blue designs and with beads and quills and long fringes made by Amatze, a Kiowa woman who had been his wife and who had been very satisfactory until she had taken her child one day and drowned them both because he would not let her go back to her Kiowa husband.

It was an hour before he was satisfied with his appearance. He left his teepee and made his way toward the fire, very proud that he could walk erect and without help.

Wading in Still Water's husband, Fights with a Knife, met him and escorted him to the seat of honor—a folded antelope skin near the center fire. He stood for a moment, and Fights with a Knife made a few remarks to tell of some of Tuchubarua's legendary exploits. They all clapped their hands, and Tuchubarua, pleasantly excited, took his seat, helped by Fights with a Knife's strong young arms.

The warriors were in all their finery, with beads and quills and long, colored fringes, and Tuchubarua was acutely conscious of the fact that his own fringes had long since been used for bullet patches in the old smooth-bore guns that had come from the Spaniards. Nevertheless, he was pleased to be there; it was the most ceremonious treatment he had had in a long, long time. He took the pipe handed to him by Fights with a Knife, puffed four times, and handed it back to Fights with a Knife. Around the fires the warriors were grouped in the first rank, with their wives and children beyond them. The wives were also dressed in their best; Quahuaha-cante's head wife was in white buckskin—a luxury of which not many Comanche wives could boast.

Fights with a Knife signaled to Wading in Still Water, and she called to three other Comanche women, and they got branches and began to dig into the coals. Then Wading in Still Water clapped her hands, and all were silent for a moment. "Ekar-raw-ro will serve the tongue," she said.

There were murmurs of approval. Black Antelope, handsome in a smoked deerskin jacket, looked modestly at the fire, very pleased and very proud. Then Tuchubarua turned his eyes to Quahuahacante and saw the evil in the warrior's face, and was glad that Ekarraw-ro was already promised.

With a little stir among those around the fire, Ekarraw-ro came from the teepee, wearing a beautiful white buckskin dress with many beads and colored designs. She was truly a *naibi*—a lovely young girl dressed in her best finery. Her eyes were aglow, but her face was grave as she faced Wading in Still Water and waited.

Wading in Still Water said: "If any man here has had relations with this woman, let him speak."

There was silence around the fire, and old Tuchubarua, with his eyes on Ekarraw-ro, began a quiet smile of pride. But a voice was heard, and Tuchubarua went cold when he heard the first sound of it.

"I have," said Quahuahacante. "I have had relations with her."

Wading in Still Water stared at Quahuahacante, dumbfounded. Tuchubarua looked at the evil eyes and would have killed the man if it had been in his power. He would have wiped the evil smirk from the man's face with a red-hot tomahawk; he would have cut off the top of his head and spilled his brains into the fire; he would have . . . but he was an old man, a very old man.

Ekarraw-ro was staring at Quahuahacante, and Tuchubarua knew from her expression of incredulity that she was innocent, that Quahuahacante had lied. But the lie had been delivered, and the Comanches would accept it at face value unless some dramatic denial could be made. That could hardly come from Ekarraw-ro, for she was only a woman, while Quahuahacante was a warrior and had many horses and very great power.

Quahuahacante continued to stare at her, and gradually Ekarraw-ro's eyes dropped to the ground—not in admission, Tuchubarua knew, but in embarrassment, in helplessness.

Black Antelope stared at Ekarraw-ro. His copper-colored face had lost its pride, and now he looked hurt and puzzled.

There was no sound around the fire. Tuchubarua looked at Quahuahacante and called on all of his ancient knowledge of Comanche ways. There could be only one answer to Quahuahacante's accusation. The Comanches had no medicine man to test a girl's virginity as did some tribes. For a girl in Ekarraw-ro's position now there was only shame that she had claimed to be something she was not. Unless someone could reveal Quahuahacante's vanity, his envy, his pettiness, in such a way as to disgrace him— unless somebody could reveal the smallnesses of character that every Comanche knew were compatible with lying, Ekarraw-ro would be forever scorned.

And Tuchubarua, to the best of his knowledge, was the only one who knew enough about Quahuahacante's weaknesses to reveal him for what he was. It would not be enough to call him a liar, for Quahuahacante's egotism would enable him to counteract it. It had to be something dramatic and something abhorrent—something, that, once revealed, would invoke Comanche disapprobation so strongly that not even Quahuahacante, with his vanity and his great power, would have the courage to stand against it.

Tuchubarua's ancient eyes searched the face of every warrior there, and he knew that none of those had the knowledge to face down Quahuahacante— none but himself. He looked around the circle, at the women there, and considered the price he would have to pay if he should undertake the task. He glanced at Quahuahacante and visualized the price the warrior would have to pay—for no man with power could make false accusation with impunity. Power itself was based on honor and integrity, and surely Quahuahacante must have offended many of his medicines with those few words. Power, however, was something like public opinion—if, indeed, it was *not* public opinion. Power might be defied as long as one could keep the knowledge to oneself. Not all men, by any means, could so defy it, but an egotistic one like Quahuahacante probably could.

Tuchubarua kept his old eyes on the warrior. What a chain of circumstances had put him in this position! It was almost as if he had lived a hundred and twenty-six years for this moment. If he had not been guest of honor at the feast, he could not have spoken out before them, because he had long ago forfeited his position and his rights. But now, at this moment, all things came together, and he knew what power he had over Quahuahacante, if he should be willing to pay the price. He tried to warn Quahuahacante with his mind, and said calmly: "Be sure you have the right to speak of this maiden, Quahuahacante."

But Quahuahacante did not hear the warning, or did not heed it. With a sneer on his lips, he said: "No right is needed, Tsukup. She has walked with me on the prairie at night . . . many times."

The man's manner was such that even Tuchubarua, for a moment, almost believed him. But he looked at Ekarraw-ro and saw the red blush that covered her face and neck, and knew it was not from guilt. He considered. He could not ask her for the truth, because a woman's word was nothing. Suddenly he felt, indeed, old and tired, for the thing he must do was roaring at him like a stampeded herd. The end would be tragedy for both of them, and it could so easily have been avoided— but now it had gone too far, and must run its tragic course. His thin lips moved. "I say you lie," he said, "and I will prove it."

Quahuahacante's face suddenly blanched; for the first time, apparently, he realized what Tuchubarua could do to him. "Be silent, Old Man!" he shouted, and leaped to his feet. "Keep your tongue in your mouth, Tsukup!"

Tuchubarua held his eyes while he got slowly to his own feet. "Quahuahacante, you cannot testify against this girl, for your word is no good. You are filled with bad thoughts and vile motives. You have violated Comanche laws. You are unclean!"

For a moment there was dead silence around the fire. Then Quahuahacante said coldly: "Old Man, I will kill you if you say a word against me."

He was fighting desperately against what Tuchubarua had to say, but Tuchubarua was not moved.

"I am going to tell the men what you have done," he said clearly, only sorry that his voice broke a little on the last word, for he had decided, and there was no going back, and the decision was as strong in him as if he had been twenty, "and they will see that you are not fit to speak against any human being."

Quahuahacante's eyes blazed in fury, and he started to move.

But Tuchubarua stood his ground and shook his head. He had made his decision to violate his own medicine, and so he did not fear to reach out for a moment of heroics and, perhaps, vainglory. "Will the great warrior Quahuahacante attack a defenseless and helpless old man?" he asked.

It was a perfect answer to Quahuahacante's threat, for now Quahuahacante would not dare.

Tuchubarua clutched the dried horned toad within his worn buckskin shirt. "I have power. It is not a great power, but it is enough to protect me." He did not explain that it would protect only his good name, for no man ever told any of the secrets of his power. Tuchubarua drew a deep breath and looked around the circle. "This man who would speak against an innocent girl . . . you all know him. You know there is something strange in his eyes. You know there is an evil spirit gnawing at his brain. And I will tell you what that demon is." He looked at Hichapat, sitting with his cane across his withered legs, and he knew Hichapat was wondering what was to come next. He looked at Black Antelope, who was staring at Ekarraw-ro, hurt as only a young man can be hurt in his vanity over the girl he loves.

Tuchubarua breathed deeply as he looked back at Quahuahacante. This was the time to reveal what he knew, to expose the evil man before him. Tuchubarua would offend his power, and his power would break him, but not even Quahuahacante with all his self-conceit could stand before Tuchubarua's knowledge without himself being broken. Tuchubarua spoke. "Many years ago," he said, "I was on my last raid . . . a war party against the Pawnees along the Padoucah Fork. This man, this Quahuahacante, was on that raid, too. It was his first, for he was only fifteen summers old."

He looked at Quahuahacante then, and saw the man sit back down, sullen, resentful, but held to his place by the force of the tribal beliefs, against which no man had the strength to stand. He knew what was coming and was trying to fight against it, but he was without strength against the certain knowledge that Tuchubarua *knew*.

Tuchubarua looked at Quahuahacante and then above him at Sits by Herself, standing back of her brother. Tuchubarua looked back at Quahuahacante. Tuchubarua could have sat down then, but he did not. He remembered the restriction on his power, but he stayed on his feet; he would spare no effort to destroy the accusation.

He had always been small of frame, and now he was somewhat shrunken, and he would need the advantage of talking on his feet. For violating the restriction, his power would destroy him—and he did not want to die, but his great love for Ekarrawro, the image of his Shoshoni wife, and his respect for honor and his contempt for Quahuahacante—all those combined in him to give him the strength to violate deliberately the restriction of his own power.

"On that raid," said Tuchubarua, "this man took his sister to care for his shield. But he was not satisfied with that. His evil desires ruled him as such desires should rule no Comanche. He violated the most sacred taboo in Comanche customs. He slept with his sister. He walked with her naked on the prairie! He committed incest! *He has maggots on his penis!*"

Every shocked eye turned back to Quahuahacante. For a moment he stared furiously at Tuchubarua, but Tuchubarua called on all the strength and knowledge of his many years, and held his eyes, and felt no wavering in his mind.

Then Quahuahacante began to shrink before the awful weight of the accusation. He became unable to face Tuchubarua. His flaming eyes lost their indignation and dropped slowly, and he stared at the ground, now stripped of all pretense, helpless in spite of all his power, in this final hour bearing the horrendous burden of his long-concealed guilt.

Tuchubarua glanced then at Sits by Herself and saw her looking down at her brother, a strange, bitter, almost triumphant smile on her face. He looked around the fire. There was a stunned silence among the Comanches. Then, as they saw that Quahuahacante admitted his guilt, indignation began to grow among them like a great black cloud. The terrible force of the tribal condemnation arose and took ominous shape, and finally, like a crushing wave, rolled out across the fire and engulfed the man who had defied it.

\* \* \*

Tuchubarua was an old, old man, and he was dying. On the day after the Buffalo Tongue Feast, Ekarraw-ro came with a large piece of hot tongue wrapped in rawhide. He inhaled the savory odor as he raised himself in the dim light of the teepee and smiled at her. "What now of Quahuahacante?" he asked.

"That evil one! This morning he planted his lance in the ground and ran against it and impaled himself on the point. But you, Grandfather, are you sick?"

"I offered insult to my medicine," he said, and shook his head slowly. "Power is a dangerous thing . . . even a small power." His ancient eyes turned to her, and he smiled. "Send Wading in Still Water, so I can give her my answer." He watched her blush, and continued to smile. Then he paused to breathe painfully, for he knew his power was closing in. "There is *pah'mo* in my *awyawt*," he said. "Fill my pipe, gentle Kaku, and leave me here in peace, for I have many, many memories."

She filled his pipe in silence, and it seemed to him she took a long time, but finally she gave it to him, with a light from the nearest fire, and then she stood in the opening of his teepee. It would not have been Comanche-like for her to make a display of her gratitude, but she said: "The Comanches will always remember the man who faced down the powerful Quahuahacante." She hesitated. Tears dropped onto the hard clay, and she whispered softly: "Good bye, Grandfather Out of the Past."

He died, but not alone, for he had had his wish.

He had lived out his days with his own people, and for him there would always be plenty of buffalo and a good horse, successful raiding parties, captive women, long and weighty councils around the campfire. For him there would be always *pah'mo*.

# About the Author

**Noel M(iller) Loomis** was born in Oklahoma Territory and retained all his life a strong Southwestern heritage. One of his grandfathers made the California Gold Rush in 1849 and another was in the Cherokee Strip land rush in 1893. He grew up in Oklahoma, New Mexico, Texas, and Wyoming, areas in the American West that would figure prominently in his Western stories. Although he began contributing Western fiction to the magazine market in the late 1930s, it was with publication of his first novel, *Rim of the Caprock* (1952), that he truly came to prominence. This novel is set in Texas, the location of two other notable literary endeavors, *Tejas Country* (1953) and *The Twilighters* (1955). In these novels, as well as *West to the Sun* (1955), *Short Cut to Red River* (1958), and *Cheyenne War Cry* (1959), Loomis very precisely sets forth a time and place in frontier history and proceeds to capture the ambiance of the period in descriptions, in attitudes responding to the events of the day, and laconic dialogue that etches vivid characters set against these historical backgrounds. *Heading West* is the first collection of his Western short stories.

# NIGHT HAWK

# STEPHEN OVERHOLSER

He came to the ranch with a mile-wide chip on his shoulder and no experience whatsoever. But it was either work on the Circle L or rot in jail, and he figured even the toughest labor was better than a life behind bars. He's got a lot to learn though, and he'd better learn it fast because he's about to face one of the toughest cattle drives in the country. They've got an ornery herd, not much water and danger everywhere they look. The greenhorn the cowboys call Night Hawk may not know much, but he does know this: The smallest mistake could cost him his life.

ISBN 10: 0-8439-5840-5
ISBN 13: 978-0-8439-5840-9          $5.99 US/$7.99 CAN

# MEDICINE ROAD

# WILL HENRY

Mountain man Jim Bridger is counting on Jesse Callahan. He knows that Callahan is the best man to lead the wagon train that's delivering guns and ammunition to Bridger's trading post at Green River. But Brigham Young has sworn to wipe out Bridger's posts, and he's hired Arapahoe warrior Watonga to capture those weapons at any cost. Bridger, Young and Watonga all have big plans for those guns, but it's all going to come down to just how tough Callahan can be. He's going to have to be tougher than leather if he hopes to make it to the post...alive.

ISBN 10: 0-8439-5814-6
ISBN 13: 978-0-8439-5814-0          $5.99 US/$7.99 CAN

# TWISTED BARS

He was known as The Duster. Five times he'd been tried for robbery and murder, and five times acquitted. He'd met the most famous of gunmen and beaten them all. Before he gives it all up, he's got one battle left to fight. The Duster needs a proper burial for his dead partner, but the blustery Rev. Kenneth Lamont refuses to let a criminal rest in his cemetery. The Duster knows if he can't get what he wants one way, there's always another. And this is a plan the reverend won't like. Not one bit...

ISBN 10: 0-8439-5871-5
ISBN 13: 978-0-8439-5871-3          $5.99 US/$7.99 CAN

# THE LAST WAY STATION
## KENT CONWELL

As soon as Jack Slade and his partner, Three Fingers
Bent, arrive in the small Texas town of New Gideon,
they know no one wants them there. There's been
some rustling in the area, and folks aren't taking too
kindly to strangers. But things don't get any better
when Slade and Bent move on. The two don't get far
before a posse from New Gideon rides up, accuses
Bent of murder, and takes him back to face a judge.
Slade knows he won't have much time before his
partner hangs on a trumped-up charge, and there's
only one way he can save his friend—he'll have to
find the real killer himself!

ISBN 10: 0-8439-5928-2
ISBN 13: 978-0-8439-5928-4          $5.99 US/$7.99 CAN

# BLOOD TRAIL TO KANSAS

## ROBERT J. RANDISI

Ted Shea thinks he is a goner for sure. All the years he's worked to build his Montana spread and fine herd of prime beef means nothing if he can't sell them. And with a vicious rustler and his gang of cutthroats scaring all the hands, no one is willing to take to the trail. Until Dan Parmalee drifts into town. A gunman and gambler with a taste for long odds, he isn't about to let a little hot lead part him from some cold cash. But it doesn't take Dan long to realize this isn't just any run. This is a...*Blood Trail to Kansas*.

ISBN 10: 0-8439-5799-9
ISBN 13: 978-0-8439-5799-0                    $5.99 US/$7.99 CAN